A Fiction Lover's Devotional

# 21 Days
## of Grace

Stories that
Celebrate God's
Unconditional
Love

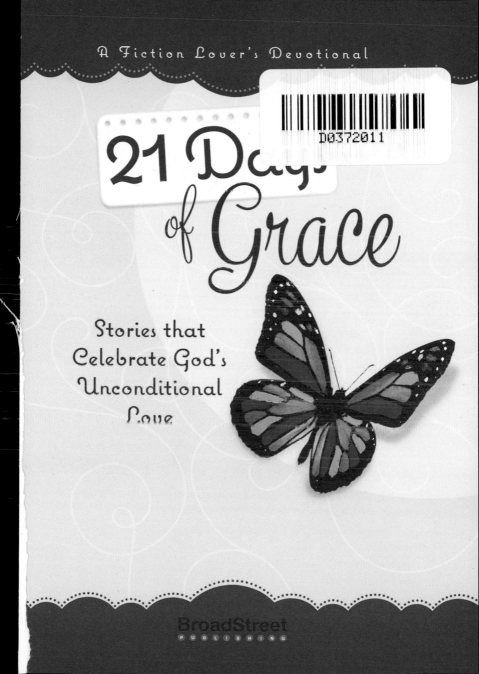

BroadStreet
PUBLISHING

Published by BroadStreet Publishing Group, LLC
Racine, Wisconsin, USA
www.broadstreetpublishing.com

# 21 Days of Grace
## Stories that Celebrate God's Unconditional Love

ISBN: 978-1-4245-5023-4 (hardcover)
ISBN: 978-1-4245-5026-5 (e-book)

Stock or custom editions of BroadStreet Publishing titles may be purchased in bulk for educational, business, ministry, fundraising, or sales promotional use. For information, please e-mail info@broadstreetpublishing.com.

Printed in China

15 16 17 18 19 20   5 4 3 2 1

# Contents

# Foreword

by Rene Gutteridge

*J*'ve always believed that fiction stories are living, breathing things. They are created, and once they are set loose, they seem to take on lives of their own. Sometimes they transfix on a soul that is willing to let them in, and it seems that every word on the page was written uniquely for the person reading it.

A story's ability to weave itself into even the hardest of hearts awes me. And as a storyteller, I'm constantly amazed at the transforming power of words. How can a simple story change the course of a human's journey? How do stories present new perspectives to people who are set in their ways?

I've witnessed one story do many things to many people. I write a story, intending on its theme and message to be this or that, and then to my surprise it has multiple veins flowing with its own life-giving supplies, some of which I never dreamed up and, as its creator, never imagined could be.

I certainly play it cool when I hear about various readers' adventures with my stories. I nod and pretend I knew all along that this work of art would do what they've told me it has done. I smile and thank them and wish them well. But as I walk away, I marvel at what my little story did after it left my care, grew up, and made its way into the world.

In my own life, I've been taken captive by many stories, but none more than the parables told by Jesus. I've read them many times over the years. Sometimes they will leap off the page, as suddenly and beautifully as a deer. The story that I thought I knew inside and out grabs my attention with ideas I never even realized were there. It plants truths and perspectives in my mind and heart that I didn't understand before. What once was ordinary becomes extraordinary. A story I've known since childhood is all at once dancing in front of me, a spectacle so astonishing that I dare not blink. I make my heart listen intently. I don't want to miss even the tiniest detail. Just minutes ago these were just tales told long ago. Now they are answers to questions that I had resolved would never be unlocked.

And all of this comes from the imagination. Even Jesus had an imagination. In fact, He is the creator of imagination, being the first creator of all things. To read a story as a human being is certainly an event, but to read a story, any story, with the Holy Spirit in our hearts gives power to thoughts that we can't reach on our own. When we open that door, there is no limit to the impact a single story can make.

Watch out for these tiny words, for those unremarkable sentences, sitting innocently and quietly on the pages of this book. Today they are just that. But in a blink of an eye, these stories may change the course of your entire life.

Rene Gutteridge is the award-winning and best-selling author of twenty-four novels in the suspense and comedy genres. She has novelized six screenplays and movies. She is a creative consultant on *Boo*, a script based on her novel series, which is in development at Sodium Entertainment. Find more about Rene at her website, renegutteridge.com.

# 1

# Through a Dark Glass

by Cindy Woodsmall

*J*va's heart pounded as she read the notice in *The Budget* about her little sister's upcoming wedding. Maybe Josiah was right. She shouldn't have the weekly Amish newspaper mailed to her. Fighting tears, she closed the paper and tucked it away in a side table.

*Focus on today and on the ministry God has given this family.*

Autumn sunlight stretched across the tiny living room, showcasing every bit of dust in the air above the open boxes scattered around the carpeted floor. Iva had been going through the cardboard boxes, and organizing their contents by category, all morning. So many people from various churches in other states had donated to the cause of helping the poor in the Appalachian Mountains of Kentucky. As Iva wiped her sweaty forehead with the back of her wrist, she whispered a prayer of thankfulness. For the donations and for the distraction.

The work was tedious, but Iva was desperate to stay pre-occupied. Anything to help her avoid dwelling on the high price she and Josiah had paid for doing what they felt God leading them to do.

As she removed toys from a box, sorting them by age and gender, the differences between these toys and those treasured by the Amish tugged at her heart. Barbie dolls had faces … and sparkly dresses with matching high heels … and curves. So unlike the cloth doll she'd played with as a little girl: faceless, with a solid pale-blue dress and a white prayer kapp covering yellow yarn pulled back in a bun.

Disco Barbie seemed to scowl at her. *You broke your vow. You did it thoughtfully and intentionally. You've betrayed your people.*

When Iva and Josiah were barely twenty-one, they'd gone through the weeks of instructions to join the Amish church. Then they'd taken their vows and were baptized according to the Ordnung—the rules by which the Old Order Amish lived. That autumn they were married in her parents' home. Fourteen months later, she gave birth to their first child.

A year after Mark was born, the pastor of a nearby non-Plain church invited her and Josiah to join them for an in-home Bible study. As they began to read the Word on their own, their hearts were stirred as if they'd been set on fire, and a desire to follow wherever God called them took root.

"*Gut* job, boys." Her husband's voice jolted Iva from her self-condemnation as he came through their front door.

Josiah walked into the house, carrying an armful of coats

and blankets. Two adorable shadows followed in his footsteps, similarly laden. He dropped the items onto the couch, and his sons mimicked the same move. Then they each wrapped their arms around one of Josiah's legs, and he marched around, toting them across the carpeted floor. The boys laughed almost as much as their dad.

Josiah glanced up, spotting the doll in Iva's hands—and, no doubt, the unshed tears in her eyes. He put his sons' feet on the floor, aimed them toward the back door, and gave them each a light pat on the backside. "Now, go out and enjoy this beautiful fall day."

They ran outside, giggling and shouting.

"Hey, you." Josiah lumbered to her, a gentle smile lifting his lips.

"Hi." She lowered her eyes and fidgeted with the doll's sequined jacket.

He hooked a finger under her chin and eased her face upward. "We weren't wrong to leave, Iva." How many times did he need to encourage her in an attempt to prevent the heartache from swallowing her?

Tears trickled down her cheeks. "I know." And she did. But it didn't matter who was right or wrong. Her heart was crushed. She hadn't seen or heard from any member of her family in two years.

Iva wiped the tears from her face. "If only they could find it in themselves to listen, to at least hear our hearts in the matter …" They should be preparing for her sister's wedding with the rest of the family, not apart from them. So very far apart.

"Maybe one day they will." His soft voice was barely above a whisper. "And if that day comes, we'll embrace them. But right now, all they have for us are unyielding opinions, fears that God will punish us, and judgments for us based on the Ordnung."

Josiah had put tremendous effort into being a peacemaker with their families. But nothing short of him and Iva remaining Amish, and repenting for even thinking about leaving, would satisfy their families.

She and Josiah had talked through all of this multiple times, and she understood it. They had seasons when peace and laughter overflowed in their hearts, but mostly she fought the pain of missing her family—and every friend she'd grown up with. She continually wanted to scream at them, *It didn't have to end this way!*

Josiah wasn't allowed to have any contact with his family either. Whenever he dealt with bouts of anger due to the harsh words and the weight of isolation, she'd been the voice of reason for him, just like he was doing for her now.

Would they ever find lasting peace over what they'd done in God's name ... and what had been done to them in His name? Her parents and siblings and Josiah's family were good, God-fearing folk. But in the worst of the battle, neither side had shown much tenderness or humility.

She eased from her husband's arms, opened the door to the side table, and pulled out the Amish newspaper. "Amanda Rose is getting married in three days." A lump formed in Iva's throat at the thought of her little sister, ten years younger than she, the baby of the family. Iva used to tote the tiny thing on her hip and cuddle with her at night to soothe her to sleep. Now she was getting married—and Iva would not be allowed to attend the wedding.

Josiah took the paper and set it on the sofa. "I'm sorry." He engulfed Iva in a warm embrace. "So very sorry."

She was sorry the Ordnung demanded excommunication for anyone who left. But she didn't regret the decision they'd made. They had longed to help the less fortunate both in the US and abroad. But the Ordnung didn't allow them to own a vehicle or drive, or to fly on a plane—all of which was needed in order to serve as missionaries.

A bishop had the authority to make some allowances despite the Ordnung. But the bishop they were under refused to compromise. And in the Amish culture, there was no leaving one church to attend another—not even a different Amish church.

So God's calling for Josiah and Iva had to fit inside their church and community, or they had to leave the Amish altogether. That's when they began to question the rules of the Ordnung.

After much prayer, they decided to leave the Amish—not out of anger or rebellion, but because they wanted to be free to do whatever they felt God leading them to.

Iva touched her husband's stubbly cheek. "I love our lives. I just wish the pain would ease."

"It will. Be patient." He grazed her fingers with his lips. "Now …" He glanced around the room, looking at the stacks of boxes. "What can I do to help?"

She took in a long breath and rolled up her sleeves. "Let's go through all the boxes in this room first. Then we'll drag in the others from the garage."

The hours melted like snow in late spring, and soon sunlight waned as shadows lengthened. Josiah brought in the boxes from the garage, then left to pick up dinner from the Hometown Café.

On her knees, Iva slid a knife across the sealed tape of another box. Under layers of bubble wrap lay something wrapped in newspaper. She tore the paper along the top and discovered a thick wooden frame.

As she eased the frame loose of its wrappings, she saw blue and white brush strokes forming a beautiful sky. Beneath it was a depiction of Christ returning to heaven, His back to the onlooker. Layers of white robes draped His body, contrasting with His dark, shoulder-length hair. Sunlight broke through the clouds, bathing Him in a peaceful glow.

Iva's heart palpitated and chills covered her from the top of her head to the soles of her feet. The thoughts that filled her mind felt as if Christ were talking personally to her.

*Love sacrifices for obedience. At times it appears to lose the battle. But I am love, and love never fails.*

"But God, *we* failed. Josiah and I only wanted to follow You, but we said things we shouldn't have. Ended up arguing instead of being gentle and encouraging. I'm sorry we didn't handle leaving better than we did. But now I'm so angry with the Amish faith." How many times had she confessed that?

Suddenly, she saw herself and Josiah kneeling before God's throne, His hand of protection stretched out, covering them as the Enemy hurled accusations concerning them.

*It is all covered by My grace.* The voice was powerful and authoritative, yet it soothed her to the depths of her heartache.

Was it possible that the arguments between her and Josiah and their families were covered under God's grace? She and her husband had been right to follow what they believed was God's leading. Yet they'd done so in an imperfect way, lacking in wisdom and patience, causing tremendous strife. It didn't matter who was more wrong. God's grace covered them all.

Iva still had many questions about why God would call them to leave, why the Amish needed to excommunicate those who left, and what the future held. But even without answers, peace began to heal her aching heart.

As Iva stood, a note fell from the frame. She picked it up and read her youngest sister's handwriting.

The moment I saw this picture at a yard sale, I knew it was meant for you. Be patient. God is working here to soften hearts. I am sure you will be able to visit soon.

Love you and miss you!
Mandy

Iva clutched the note to her chest, breathing deeply as tears welled. Even though God's children could only see through a dark glass until they entered eternity, His love never failed. Never.

## Life Application

Many good people have been hurt by those within their church. Even when we are trying our best to do what we believe God wants, our brothers and sisters in Christ may disagree with our goals and viewpoints, fighting us. And we lash out in response.

Those situations are grievous beyond measure. When they happen, we need to be patient with ourselves, with those who oppose us, and with the heartache and anger of the situation. This is only possible through a combination of prayer and intentional self-control.

First Corinthians 13:12 says, "For now we see through a glass, darkly; but then face to face: now I know in part; but then shall I know even as also I am known" (KJV).

### About the Author

**Cindy Woodsmall** is a *New York Times* and CBA best-selling author who has written fifteen works of fiction. Her connection with the Amish community has been widely featured in national media outlets. In 2013, the *Wall Street Journal* listed Cindy as one of the top three most popular authors of Amish fiction. Cindy and her husband reside near the foothills of the North Georgia Mountains.

# 2

# The Smallest Gift

## by Robin Bayne

Ceci watched a stream of deliveries flow into the cramped hospital room, the scent of flowers overwhelming the smell of disinfectant. It seemed every florist and courier in town had brought an arrangement, basket, or plant to Mike's room.

And Mike, poor guy, lay completely oblivious to it all. Despite monitors beeping, hoses dripping, and nurses constantly prodding him, he remained blissfully unaware of the ever-growing greenhouse that room 346B was becoming. Ceci worried whether her best friend's brother—and her childhood crush—would ever wake up and see all the gifts.

She reached over and stroked the back of his hand, making sure not to disturb any tubes. His skin felt cool. Could he hear anything? Was he aware?

Only three days earlier, Mike had been the active guy at the children's center where he worked, coordinating activities for disabled kids. He'd also been the youth group leader for his church.

No wonder so many people had sent signs of affection.

Ceci felt a slight pull in her gut. She couldn't afford to buy him anything. Well, maybe a card. But she'd have to leave the room to do that, and she didn't think Mike should be alone right now. Nurses weren't much comfort. They didn't have time to be, rushed and spread thin among so many patients. Ceci sighed and stroked Mike's forehead. It was cool too.

Mike snorted and Ceci jumped. But he settled again quickly.

She wondered what he would make of her staying by his bed all this time.

The wall clock ticked off loud moments, reminding Ceci she'd been sitting for too long. She stretched and paced the room. At the foot of the hospital bed, an electronic panel registered all kinds of data, including the patient's weight: 175 pounds. For a six-foot-one-inch guy, he was lean. She shuddered at the thought of herself possibly being in a bed like this someday, with her own weight on display for everyone to see.

She noticed Mike's high school ring on his finger, the bright blue stone sparkling from the fluorescent lighting. How strange that he lay there, broken and pale, while the jewelry looked perfect.

The other driver had just suffered bruises, Merry had said as she cried on Ceci's shoulder while they drove to St. Joseph's emergency room with Mike's parents. It had been the other guy's fault, but that was little consolation.

"Ceci!" Merry came in, then swallowed her up in a warm hug.

"There's no change."

"I know. I stopped at the nurse's station. She said you were still here. You have to go home and get some rest."

Ceci looked at Mike. She couldn't tear herself away from him for something as unimportant as sleep.

"Have you eaten?"

She shook her head.

"Let me take you to the cafeteria. Mom and Dad are on their way. They'll sit with him."

Ceci nodded, bowed her head, and asked God to watch over her friend. Then she let Merry lead her into the noisy, bright hallway. They followed yellow arrow signs to the eating area. Nothing like a school cafeteria, this place was fancy and had lots of food choices. Even dinner entrees.

Ceci selected a tuna sandwich and Merry grabbed a huge slice of pepperoni pizza. They found a small table by the window, overlooking a courtyard.

"It's so sweet of you to stay with him, but I have to insist you go home for some rest. And a shower." Merry winked and took a big bite, holding her slice with both hands.

Ceci felt her cheeks warming. Did she stink? Yikes! "I will, I promise. I just can't imagine how he would feel if he woke up and no one was there."

Merry nodded. "We appreciate that you've been picking up the slack for when my family can't be here, and we love you for it. But the hospital will call us. And he'll see all those flowers and know that people were thinking of him."

"True. But—"

"No buts. I'm serious. You need some sleep."

Ceci appreciated her friend's concern. "Okay. But I'll be back tomorrow."

"I know you will."

She sent up a silent prayer of thanks that at least this had happened in summer, while she was on break from her job as a teacher.

On their way back to Mike's room, they were nearly run over by a delivery guy bearing flowers and silver helium balloons.

"Sorry," he muttered, pushing into 346B. "Looks like a hothouse exploded in here."

Merry and Ceci exchanged glances. They would have laughed if the situation weren't so grim.

But Mike still slept.

After three days, Ceci and Mike's family had settled into a routine. Ceci stayed with him during the day while the others worked. Merry and her parents came and went as they could. The beeps of the monitors became part of Ceci's very thought patterns, and the smell of disinfectant took up permanent residence in her nose.

She held Mike's hand, talked to him, and read to him from the Bible and other books and magazines, just in case he was able to listen. She was glad he didn't have a roommate.

The nurses brought her water and meals when they could. The flower deliveries slowed but kept arriving. Ceci added her own get-well card to the narrow dresser in the room.

After she finished a supper of bland chicken, green beans, and some sort of mystery soup, Ceci prayed over Mike and then settled in for a read-aloud session with a new suspense novel. She tried to use different voices for the various characters, and gradually found herself getting involved in the story.

"Ceci!" Merry's mother's shrill voice made her jump. "Sweetheart, that's so wonderful of you to read to him!" The woman pulled Ceci into a hug, then turned her toward a lady she hadn't met. "This is Mike's aunt Eleanor, my husband's sister. Eleanor, this is Ceci Carrollton, Merry's dearest friend." She leaned close to Ceci and whispered, "I have to run to the store for some personal items. Could you please entertain her for a little while?"

When they were alone, the gray-haired woman gave Ceci a harsh stare that made her squirm. "So, you were reading to my nephew?"

Ceci explained her theory that he might be able to hear and process what was going on.

"Nonsense," Eleanor snapped. "You're wasting your time." She glanced around the room. "So many flowers! Which ones are from you?"

Ceci looked down, even though she knew she had nothing to be ashamed of. "I brought a card." She lamely pointed. Why did she feel so defensive?

"But you're Merry's best friend, right?"

She stood straighter. "Yes, I am."

"Hmm." Eleanor brushed past her and leaned over the bed, stroking Mike's cheek and forehead. "May we have a private moment?"

"Sure. I'll be in the hall if you need me."

"I won't."

Ceci's face flamed as she fled, her stomach in knots. Why did she let people get to her? That old woman had no idea how she felt about Mike. Or all the ways she had helped him and his family.

Maybe her efforts weren't enough. Did Mike's family need to see lavish displays of pretty, shiny objects to believe that she cared?

Merry's mom returned, clutching a paper bag. "Are you feeling okay, dear?"

"Not really. I think I'm going to head home. Give Merry my love." She rushed to the elevator before the woman could respond.

Ceci didn't really feel like going to the hospital the next morning. But she didn't want to let the family down. So she bribed herself with flavored coffee, crawled out of bed, got dressed, and drove into town.

The room was buzzing with visitors, most of whom greeted Ceci warmly. Eleanor glanced down her nose at her. Ignoring the cold woman, Ceci went to Mike's side. When she squeezed his hand, she could almost convince herself that she felt him squeeze back. But a quick check of his eyes showed no change.

She sighed, turned back to the others, and made a bit of polite small talk. Ceci wished they would all leave so she could read to Mike some more. She had practiced a new voice for the story's villain and wanted to try it out.

After an hour of attempting to maintain pleasantries, Ceci needed a break. She announced she was going to the gift shop and made her way to the lobby.

She browsed the display shelves, considering a few small items she could afford to buy for Mike. But it felt shallow to do that. He had so many extravagant presents already. Ceci wanted to give him a non-material gift: her time. She was fortunate to have a career that allowed that.

She purchased a bottle of soda, then returned to the elevator. She'd spend another hour with Mike and then take off.

When the elevator dinged at the third floor, she emerged to cheering from the end of the hall near Mike's door.

Ceci hurried, her soda swishing.

Merry sprang from the room. "Ceci, he's awake! Come on!" She tugged Ceci inside and they elbowed past the crowd of people, all chatting excitedly. Mike's mom was bent over him, stroking his hair.

Ceci hovered at the foot of the bed, eager to see Mike awake but not wanting to intrude on the family.

Merry took her hand. "Come say hi."

Ceci swallowed hard, then took a step toward Mike.

"Clear the way, please." A tall doctor in scrubs pushed through the doorway.

"Everyone out," ordered the nurse who followed him.

Visitors poured out of the room. Ceci lingered in a corner as everyone else left.

The doctor approached Mike. "So, young man, how are you feeling?" he asked as the nurse took his vital signs.

"I'm not sure," Mike said, his voice quiet and raspy.

The nurse beamed. "A lot of friends and relatives have been waiting for you to wake up." She gestured toward the plants and gifts. "You're a much-loved young man."

Mike's gaze took in the colorful arrangements around him.

Embarrassed, Ceci slunk toward the door.

"Ceci!" Mike's voice cracked from lack of use. "Wait."

She froze near the doorway.

"Please come here."

The nurse nodded at Ceci. She crept toward the bed.

Mike reached for her hand, his grip warm and stable. "I need you to stay." His blue eyes glimmered. "After all," he whispered, speaking in the voice of her suspense novel's villain, "we have to find out who the bad guy is."

Ceci chuckled, her eyes filling with tears. "Yes, we do."

## Life Application

Have you ever felt like you weren't buying enough things, giving enough presents, or spending enough money to keep up with those around you? The perceived need for expensive things is a slippery slope that ends in feeling trapped.

Perhaps you've been fortunate enough to be able to send lavish gifts to friends or loved ones ... only to still feel empty afterward.

When my grandmother was declining from the last stages of Parkinson's disease, I mailed her many greeting cards—some with Bible verses, others with pretty pictures or my own notes, anything I thought might provide her with a glimmer of hope. Whenever I dropped one in the mailbox, I pictured her smiling as she spied one of my envelopes in her daily mail. I knew she shared my faith and the hope that came with it.

My work commitments didn't leave me as much time as I would have liked to spend with her at the assisted-living home, but I took small gifts whenever I did visit. She appreciated the occasional box of chocolates, but we both enjoyed the cards more.

There will never be enough material goods in this world to satisfy our need for faith, hope, and love. But sometimes all three can be found in the smallest of gestures.

## About the Author

**Robin Bayne** is the author of Christian and "sweet" romance, including the Carol Award–winning *The Artist's Granddaughter*. She compiled a collection of devotionals for writers, *Words to Write By*, featuring work by many well-known Christian authors. She lives in Maryland with her husband of twenty-four years and works a day job in community bank lending.

# 3

# True Confession

by Angela Elwell Hunt

*In this excerpt from the novel* Charles Towne, *a seven teenth-century pirate is suffering from guilt brought on by his rash actions. Tormented by the deaths of inno- cent people, sea captain Trace Bettencourt cut himself off from friends, family, and love. On one of his jour- neys, he and his first mate, Duncan, encounter Rachelle Bailie and her servant, Virtue.*

As Duncan settled the women and began digging a fire pit on the beach, Trace wandered away, osten- sibly to search for firewood. The scrubby palmettos gave way almost immediately to tall, thin pines, and he wan- dered among them for ten minutes without pausing, lost in his thoughts.

What in the world had Rachelle intended? Like a foolish,

impetuous female she had leapt off that ship and into the water, knowing he would be forced to come after her.

He shook his head, smiling despite himself. In all his days on the sea, he had never met anyone with such blind faith … in him.

Why had she done it? Why did she believe in him? He hadn't done anything particularly brave on her behalf. He had promised to see her safely to Roxbury, and he couldn't very well abandon her now, especially in the bowels of a ship commanded by a scoundrel like Pinckert. That little toad would not have hesitated to hang Rachelle and Virtue from the yardarms, if—

Trace stopped on the path as everything went silent within him. If Rachelle hadn't jumped overboard, they'd all be swinging from the yardarms now, their faces purpling above a hanging noose. Trace had hoped Pinckert would submit easily, but in that instant when their eyes met above his pistol, he realized the Englishman wouldn't capitulate.

Cold air brushed across the backs of his legs, and his scalp tingled. Trace sank to a fallen log on the ground, then lowered his head and ran his hand through his hair.

*Oh, God, help me. I nearly killed all of us.*

He felt himself flush with shame, but the rising emotion was the mere tip of a long seam of guilt that snaked its way back through the years. His guilt was his cross to bear, and though he had prayed for forgiveness, *begged* God for understanding, the load had never been lightened.

He had sought God in chapels and lain awake under the

stars, pouring out his heart to the Master of the universe. Though some part of him hoped that Christ's forgiveness included mercy enough to allow holy absolution, during his solitary confession Trace had never felt any emotion but despair.

Did he confess only to himself? Sometimes he felt as though his prayers went no higher than his hat. Prayer brought him no relief from pain; the haunting sorrows and hurts of his past still festered. Though he would never admit his feelings even to Duncan, Trace could not forget his sin or put it behind him.

One minister Trace consulted told him to take forgiveness by faith. Not wanting to sin further by calling God a liar, Trace did his best to believe the Almighty had forgiven him, but he could not escape his misery and bitterness. Forgiven or not, he was still an outcast and a wanted man.

He clasped his hands as he looked up at the tall trees soaring overhead. Perhaps God had forgiven his sin and kept the memory of it alive for a purpose.

A few months ago, Trace would not have minded a life of solitude, but then Rachelle had entered his world, blinding him with beauty and sweetness he would never possess, stinging him with temptations of softness he could never claim.

"There must be something more." His eyes fell to the velvet shadows at his feet. Thick snaking roots covered the ground; the interwoven pines shaded his head, sheltering him in a perfect forest cathedral.

But for him, it was wasted beauty. Either forgiveness was

some sort of spiritual ticket to heaven, no more and no less, or Trace was not worthy of the forgiving grace of God.

*Later, Trace and Rachelle meet her long-lost father, Mojag, missionary to the Indians.*

Trace and the minister were alone. Silence fell between them, broken only by the sound of the Indians' distant voices and the wind in the pines.

Mojag took a deep breath and stood upon the wagon bed, planting his feet with battleship solidity. The forest around him was dense with blue shadows and the promise of dawn. His face, resolute and strong, shimmered in the half-light. "Trace Bettencourt," he said, his eyes shiny as if with dreams. "The Spirit of the Lord bids you to stop running. Where shall you go from His Spirit? Where shall you flee from His presence? If you ascend up into heaven, God is there. If you make your bed in hell, behold He is there. If you take the wings of the morning, and dwell in the uttermost parts of the sea, even there shall His hand lead you and His right hand shall hold you. Psalm 139 promises so."

Mojag fell silent for a moment, applauded by the fluttering evergreens and the quiet sigh of the river. Even the Indians, whose voices had filled the woods a few moments before, seemed to listen in silence.

"Aye," Trace answered, hot tears filling his eyes. "God

haunts me. I know He follows me everywhere, for I can feel His presence. It is His forgiveness I have never felt, though I have often sought it."

"Why shouldn't He give it to you?" Mojag's stentorian voice rumbled through the forest. "The Lord is merciful and gracious, slow to anger, and plenteous in mercy. He will not always chide, neither will He keep His anger forever. He has not dealt with us after our sins, nor rewarded us according to our iniquities."

Trace turned on the minister in a sudden flash of defensive spirit. "Don't you think I've heard this before? I know everything you're saying, but nothing changes the fact that I do not feel forgiven. I've committed serious sins, malfeasance and mutiny and murder. I've begged God to forgive me, to cover me in His grace and allow me to make a new start, and yet I rise up from my knees with the same shadows on my soul, the same price upon my head."

Trace's outburst had startled Mojag, but now the minister's face settled into lines of satisfaction. "You are well on your way to forgiveness," he said, his voice soft. "The admitting of evil is the first beginning of good. What you need, my friend, is to make confession."

Trace snorted. "I'm not a Catholic."

Mojag lowered himself so that he sat directly in front of Trace. "Sometimes we privately confess ourselves in the dark, but our sins remain hidden; they still fester in our souls. But if you confess yourself to a brother, your sin is uncovered and brought out into the light. Though God's forgiveness is genuine whether you seek Him privately or publicly, the heat of the light destroys pride … and may help you find the peace you are seeking."

Mojag Bailie was an unusual clergyman, and this was the most unorthodox teaching Trace had ever heard. But it made sense. Perhaps pride had held him back. He had been so conscious of his position as captain that he'd never been able to speak openly about his guilt to anyone—until Rachelle.

After a long moment, he nodded. "All right. How do we do it?"

Mojag smiled with beautiful candor. "You talk. I listen."

Trace let his head fall back and stared at the slowly brightening sky. "It all began years ago, when I allowed Duncan to kill my captain."

Mojag and Trace had been sitting in the wagon for over an hour. Though Rachelle heard the deep rise and fall of Trace's voice, she could not catch his words.

The sound stopped, and during a long moment of silence, Rachelle crept forward. Trace now hunched in the wagon with his head bowed, and Mojag had risen to his knees. His broad hands rested upon Trace's gleaming hair; his face looked toward heaven. His mouth moved in words Rachelle couldn't understand, but she saw Trace's shoulders shaking as Mojag prayed.

Did he weep with sorrow or joy? She crept closer, wanting to be near if Trace needed her.

"The fear and pride that clung to you like barnacles cling to others also," Mojag was saying as she walked toward them. "You are not alone in your sin, nor are you alone in forgiveness. Break free of your guilt, Trace Bettencourt. The cleansing grace of God flows to you."

Trace lifted his face and opened his eyes. Rachelle saw tears running down his cheeks, glittering like jewels in the sunlight. She ran to the wagon and climbed in, crawling to his side as he reached out for her.

Emotions—his, Rachelle's, Mojag's—hung thick in the air like smoke, but Trace could not find words to express them. He had cut himself off too many times to speak easily.

"Trace Bettencourt," Mojag said, seeming to follow Trace's thoughts, "God has forgiven you. Now you must forgive yourself."

Today there were no shadows across his heart, for his soul had filled with a fathomless peace and the light of freedom. It was time to accept forgiveness … and love.

"Rachelle—" He pulled out of her embrace and looked at her, his eyes probing to her very soul. "I told you once to search your heart. If you will do it again, and if you find me there, know that I will always love you. If you would take me as I am, I would give my life to you."

Rachelle placed her hands on Trace's arms. "You once said"—her eyes watered in the sunlight—"that when I could give you a new name, a new face, and a new soul, you would be good enough to please me. But I like your name, Trace Bettencourt. I would not change your face or a hair upon your head, and I believe you have found healing for your soul. I will take you as you are, and I would give my life to you in return."

Rachelle closed her eyes and kissed the pirate who had stolen her heart … and finally brought her home.

## Life Application

Have you ever committed a wrong for which you can't seem to find forgiveness? Perhaps it was something as simple as a comment that deeply wounded someone; maybe it was something as significant as abortion. Perhaps your sin is something you've never shared with the people who know you best. Maybe you've never even gathered the courage to discuss it with the Lord, who knows you completely.

If God is God, He knows all about it, doesn't He? And if He is love, surely He forgives, right? Do not despair, my friend. No sin is beyond the reach of His cleansing mercy.

Then why does this secret from your past continue to haunt your dreams and idle moments? Perhaps, like Trace, pride and fear stand between you and freedom. If you speak to the Lord, He will listen. God always rewards confession with grace and mercy.

## About the Author

**Angela Hunt** is the best-selling author of more than one hundred works ranging from picture books to nonfiction to novels. In 2007, her novel *The Note* was featured as a Christmas movie on the Hallmark channel. Romantic Times Book Club presented her with a Lifetime Achievement Award in 2006.

# 4

# Promptly at Seven

## by Barbara Curtis

6:40 p.m., and the corner window table was still occupied. Pierre hadn't even taken their dessert order yet.

He stepped to the server station, planted his feet at a forty-five-degree angle, hands behind his back, and waited. How long would the young couple hold hands and stare into each other's eyes? He needed that table by seven. Yet he couldn't intrude on an engagement dinner at La Fleur.

Of course he wanted their night to be exceptional. But Lila and her husband would be here in less than twenty minutes. If the couple ordered dessert, he wouldn't be able to clear the table, change the linens, and reset the service in time. Doubtless Miss Lila wouldn't complain about a different location after a summer of Tuesdays at the same table. But what if she were seated outside his section? He needed to be their server—tonight of all nights.

Part-time waitstaff passed by with trays, circumventing

Pierre as if he were part of the French provincial décor. The trailing scent of pineapple and mint announced the Tuesday-night lamb chop special, which Lila would order—within minutes.

The moment the adoring couple reached for their sparkling cider, Pierre hastened over, his practiced smile in place. "Miss. Sir. Have you decided which dessert you'll be celebrating your engagement with this evening?"

The girl giggled. "I'm actually pretty full."

Pierre reached inside his jacket pocket for their check. "Then may I leave—"

"How about you, Brad?" She picked up the dessert menu. "We could share something."

"Maybe."

Pierre backed away. "I'll give you a few moments to decide." Only decades of experience kept his smile intact.

He checked on another table, then looked at his watch. 6:51. Lila, though white-haired, bent, and old enough to be his mother, loved romance. She would not approve of Pierre rushing a couple through their engagement dinner just to be seated at her regular table. Maybe in another sixty years this girl would be a Lila, coming in every Tuesday, sitting at table ten, still holding hands with her husband.

Brad raised a finger.

Pierre hurried over. "Might I recommend the chocolate mousse?" That was what Lila always ordered.

He shook his head. "We decided to pass. Just the check, please."

"Of course." Pierre slipped the leather folder from his jacket and set it on the table. Brad fumbled for his wallet, then handed over a credit card.

Pierre wound past the other waitstaff with the same doggedness he'd had fifty years ago on the football field.

As soon as the couple rose and bid him good night, Pierre stripped and reset the table. He centered the vase of yellow roses at seven on the dot. Then he returned to his position and watched the front door.

Each week over the summer, Lila and her husband had arrived exactly at seven. He didn't know the man's name, only that Lila called him "darling." She always greeted Pierre warmly and engaged in conversation with him. While Mr. Darling used words sparingly, his hand often lingered on Lila's arm when he did speak.

Pierre reached into his jacket pocket and fingered the pamphlet Lila had given him last Tuesday. *God's Gift of Grace.* All week he had reread the words, mentally listing questions to ask. Of course he wouldn't interrupt their dinner conversation. But perhaps, when he brought Lila's chocolate mousse over, she would be willing to tell him more.

When he was little, his mother had told him Bible stories about Jesus. After she died, no one at the orphanage had broached the subject. Neither did anyone else. Until Lila.

The booklet made it sound like Jesus wasn't only for children. Or the religious, or the rich. That left him with a burning question. Was Jesus for even him?

Any moment now, his couple would walk in. Lila would

lean over and smell the flowers on the table. "Yellow roses are for joy and caring," she'd told him the first night they dined here. So that's what he set out for them each week.

When Mr. Darling said grace tonight, Pierre intended to stand near enough to savor the words he spoke to God.

At 7:10 the family at the table next to Lila's waved him over, and Pierre took their order. On his way to the kitchen, he detoured past the front window, hoping to see Lila and her husband walking up the street. Where could they be?

At 7:30 the maître d' insisted on seating someone at table ten. The woman who took Lila's chair shoved the vase aside and spread papers and blueprints across the linens.

Customers filtered in and out, and Pierre served each one, endeavoring to display a continuous smile. Apparently the Darlings weren't coming. He sighed. Well, surely they'd be back next week.

But they weren't. Nor did they return the following week. Or the week after that.

He had no way to contact them. He didn't even know their last name, as they never made a reservation and always paid in cash. And he'd never asked.

Shame seeped through him. All these weeks Lila had included him in conversations, showing interest in him as a person. Yet, always aware that the manager might be watching, Pierre had prided himself on maintaining a professional boundary between patron and server. Yes, those were the culprits: fear and pride.

Lila had reached out to him, but he'd waited too long to return her kindness.

Where was she now?

Each Tuesday that passed without Lila and her husband, Pierre's hope ebbed. Always he held their table as long as he could, ignoring side-glances from other waitstaff. And every week he carried the pamphlet in his jacket.

If only her God would bring her back.

One sunny Monday morning, Pierre meandered through the park before his shift. He sat on his favorite bench under a canopy of leaves, where a symphony of birds harmonized with playground laughter.

"Where do you think they are?" he asked the sparrows in the overhead branches.

How ridiculous was this, fretting over people he barely knew? But he did know them. They were prompt, and they loved routine and fine food. Lila treasured yellow roses and holding hands with her husband. And she knew God. Whatever had happened to this couple, undoubtedly they possessed the peace that booklet talked about.

A rustling mingled like a sour note with the laughter and bird songs. Pierre sat up straight. An elderly man, his shoulders slumped, shuffled along the path. As he neared the bench, Pierre recognized him and jumped up. "Sir!"

Mr. Darling looked over. "Why, Pierre. It's nice to see you. But won't you please call me Charles? We're not at the restaurant."

"Of course. Would you care to join me?" He motioned to the bench and they both sat down.

The sun glinted on twin paths of moisture drying on Charles's cheeks.

Pierre cleared his throat. "I've missed seeing you on Tuesday evenings."

He nodded. "As have we."

"May I ask about Miss Lila?"

The frail man knotted his hands. "She …" He bowed his head.

*No!* Pierre's heart pounded. *Please, no!*

Charles looked up. "She had a stroke."

"I'm so sorry to hear that. How severe was it—if I may ask?"

"The doctors say that with therapy she'll get most of her arm and leg use back. Eventually."

*Thank goodness.*

*No. Thank God!*

"I don't know what to do for her." He looked down again. "Or without her."

Pierre touched Charles's arm. Perhaps there was something *he* could do.

Pierre wheeled a cart down the hall of Oakdale Nursing Home. He knocked on Lila's door promptly at seven.

Charles greeted him with a wink. "Come in."

Lila sat in her wheelchair, her eyes sparkling. "Pierre! What a pleasant surprise!" She grasped her husband's hand. "And thank you for arranging such a wonderful treat."

"Good evening, madam. Sir." Pierre placed a yellow rose on Lila's quilted lap robe. "As this is Tuesday, tonight's special is pineapple-mint lamb chops." He set two plates on her bedside table and lifted the metal covers with a flourish.

"Oh, Pierre." Tears clouded Lila's eyes. "Thank you."

He bowed. "You are most welcome."

As the couple sat across from each other, Pierre fingered the folded paper in his pocket and forced himself to be bold. "Miss Lila, after your meal I'd like to inquire about the pamphlet you gave me."

Her face lit up. "You've read it, then?"

"Yes, ma'am."

"Oh, I'd love to tell you about it. And my darling can help if I get too tired. Right, Charles?"

"Of course." Charles pulled another chair up to the tiny table. "Why don't you join us."

"Oh, I couldn't intrude on your special dinner."

"Nonsense." Lila grinned. "This night would be even more special if you sat with us. There's plenty of food to share. And we could start answering your questions right away."

Pierre could not resist such an enticing invitation. "Thank you." Overcoming decades of stalwartly kept professional boundaries, he joined his friends at the table.

## Life Application

Do you ever think you're too ordinary to make a difference for God? Or that once you reach a certain age you have nothing to offer? Has fear or pride ever kept you from reaching out to others?

God brings people across our paths in unlikely places. At work. In restaurants. In a nursing home. No one is too old to share—or to receive—the grace of God.

"The Lord God has given Me the tongue of the learned, that I should know how to speak a word in season to him who is weary. He awakens Me morning by morning, He awakens My ear to hear as the learned" (Isaiah 50:4 NKJV).

Where will God lead you to "speak a word in season" to someone who is weary?

### About the Author

**Barbara Curtis** lives in Connecticut with her family (and two cats and a dog). She loves editing and writing, especially fiction, finding it a way to fulfill Psalm 34:3: "Oh, magnify the Lord with me, and let us exalt His name together" (NKJV).

# 5

# We Called Him Happy Face

by Cecil Murphey

They are coming! They are coming!"

Since the moment the sun peeked out from the edge of the sky, our whole village had been waiting to hear those words. Voices filled with excitement floated through the air. No one would plant maize or beans today. Instead, our minds were filled with thoughts of food, laughter, and games.

Having a visitor was always special, but this day, my brother Kana was coming home. I did not remember him. He left our village to go to school in Nairobi when I was small. Mama often spoke of her firstborn. When she mentioned Kana, her eyes glowed and her voice softened. He was special to Mama. So he was special to me.

Kuja, my older sister, saw him first. She pointed and whooped loudly to alert everyone. We all ran to the edge of our village.

Kana walked up the hill between the cassava plants, and I ran toward him. He was very tall, like Mama said. He walked like the mighty warrior I pictured when I played games with my friends.

When I saw someone following two paces behind him, I stopped. I had never seen a white man.

After entering the village, Kana greeted Mama and Papa, then my brothers Bino and Ambo. As he stood before me, I gazed into a face that spoke kindness. "So you are my little brother Oko." The firmness of his fingers clasping my shoulder showed he liked me.

"Oko, I would like you to meet my friend."

I turned and stared at the stranger with the pale skin. He wore shoes. He must have been a rich man, because only important people wore shoes.

Kana told us the white man's name, but no one in our family could make the English sounds.

"We cannot say his name." I shook my head. "We must give him a new one." In our country we sometimes changed people's names based on the way they behaved.

"He came to Kenya only four months ago," Kana said. "When he has learned our language, we will find a fitting Luo name for him."

I said nothing, but decided to watch this odd creature with eyes the color of the sky.

Just then, the white man smiled at me. I backed away in fear. Once, when I spilled some medicine, the magic doctor screamed, "You are bad! Evil spirits have taken hold of you. If you do not change, the white man will get you. White people make whips from the tail of the hippo, and they will beat you until your body is covered with blood."

Yes, I needed to watch this stranger very carefully.

The pale-skinned man went from person to person, shaking hands and smiling. One time, he smiled so big I saw that he had all of his teeth. Hmm. White people must have unusual customs.

Legend says our first chief, who had all of his teeth, could not open his mouth due to a great sickness. Because he could eat no food, he starved to death.

When I am older, I will have my six bottom front teeth removed. Then everyone will know I am of the Luo tribe and that I am now a man. And if I become sick, my family will be able to give me food. Then I will not die.

What protection do white people have? Is that not a problem for them?

The strange man and Kana entered Mama's hut. Kuja started a fire to cook the four fish she caught in Nam Lolwe and the chicken Bino killed for our feast. Mama prepared the sweet bananas and pineapples she bought yesterday at Tuesday Market. I gathered seven eggs from Kuku, our laying hen. No shame would come upon Mama for not offering a good meal to our visitor.

Our entire village enjoyed a grand feast. Afterward, Kana and the stranger went out to the thorn tree where our chief held meetings with the elders and women gathered in the evenings to jabber and laugh.

"Come," Kana called to everyone. "Hear what my friend says Good God is telling us."

I sat where I could watch the white man closely. When he saw me he smiled again. Why was this strange man always smiling?

"*Misawa*," he said.

I could not believe he had said *hello* in Luo. "You know our language?"

"*Matin tin.*" Only a few words. When he smiled again, he had the happiest face I had ever seen. Would Happy Face not make a good name for him?

Kana and Happy Face sang about Good God who loved us. The words told us not to fear this god.

In our village, we offered a goat each new moon so God of the Tall Mountain would not destroy our crops or bring sickness. How could we not fear a god who could cause so much trouble?

Another song the stranger and brother sang said that we cannot see God, yet he is with us. And he has given us a book that teaches us. I liked this song. The tune went round and round inside my head after we finished singing.

Then they sang a song about Yesu, who is also God. I frowned in confusion. How could one god be two?

Happy Face sat in front of me on Papa's favorite three-legged stool, his back to me. What strange hair—red, the color of the millet we harvested during rainy season. And thin like corn silk.

I wondered how his hair felt. I reached out and touched the back of his head. Happy Face turned around and smiled.

He picked me up and put me on his lap. I felt afraid of this pale-skinned man with so many teeth. But Papa said we must never show fear. So I stayed there.

He placed my hand in his hair. Never had I felt anything so soft—even softer than the dried sisal from which we made rope. He smiled as he watched me. Why did he do that?

When Happy Face stood to speak, he set me gently on his stool. He spoke in his foreign language while Kana translated. Long words poured forth. I yawned and drifted off to sleep.

I awakened when Happy Face picked me up. Once again, he smiled. This time he stroked my hair. The tender touch of his hand showed me he was good. Magic Doctor had lied. Happy Face would not hurt me.

My smile matched his as he sat again, with me on his lap. He smelled like the fragrant moonflowers that grew near Nam Lolwe.

Papa invited Kana and Happy Face into our hut for tea. Mama would not offer any to me, for only special visitors got this wonderful treat. But I could watch Kana and my new friend from the doorway as they drank.

Happy Face stood, but he did not put me on the ground. Instead, he carried me into the hut. Never had my heart beat with such joy.

Even before Mama entered our one-room home, the aroma teased my nose. Mama had boiled the tea with milk, sugar, and lemongrass for extra flavor. I smacked my lips as she filled each cup with the golden liquid.

Happy Face answered questions that my father asked.

Kana translated. I yawned again and almost fell asleep. But as my eyes started to close, Happy Face placed his cup to my lips. "Drink," he said in Luo.

Truly? He nodded. I sipped. Surely Mama made the best tea in the world. "Thank you, Happy Face."

Kana laughed. Papa smiled. Everyone stared at me. A puzzled look clouded the white man's eyes.

My brother spoke to him, then turned to me. "I told him you called him Happy Face in our language, and that the word you used means 'a person having much joy inside himself.' Because of his inner happiness, such a person showers happiness on others."

"Let it be so," Papa said. "Oko has given our new friend a Luo name, and it fits him well. All of us shall call him Happy Face."

After Kana translated, Happy Face thanked us in our language. Then he added, in his poorly spoken Luo, "You honor me."

More talk followed, mostly about Good God. Happy Face still held me and I felt safe.

When the sun was ready to sleep for the night, Happy Face and Kana had to leave. They promised to return and teach us more about Good God.

"I shall see you again, little friend." Happy Face shook my hand.

"Why did you hold me?" I worked up the courage to ask. "And why did you give me tea?"

After Kana translated, Happy Face smiled again. In Luo, he said, "God loves you and sent me to tell you about Jesus, who loves you very much. And I love you."

"I love you too," I said quietly.

I did not understand this God of Happy Face. I wanted very much to learn more when he returned. But I wondered … if I could see God, would He smile at me the way Happy Face did?

## Life Application

What does it take to get others to believe in Jesus Christ? Too often, we think that we need to find exactly the right words. If we say them well, that's all listeners need to embrace the faith.

But is merely speaking the proper theological words really effective? Too often our lifestyles contradict our words. How often do we hear the expression "Your actions speak so loudly I can't hear what you're saying"?

This short story came about as I reflected on my ministry in Kenya, East Africa, where I lived during the 1960s. While serving as a missionary, I realized that simply proclaiming the gospel was rarely enough to produce faith. We had to demonstrate to the nationals that the living God lived in us. Our words about loving others resonated with them only after they witnessed our compassion through our actions.

The part of the story about giving names to foreigners that matched their personalities is true, even today. A few missionaries' nicknames pointed out their lack of relationship with the nationals—even though most of those missionaries didn't know what the people were calling them.

Those of us who worked closely with the nationals

eventually learned our African nicknames. That fact, as much as anything else, made us realize that the people to whom we gave ourselves accepted us, grasped that we demonstrated what we taught, and so were willing to listen to our words.

Throughout the book of Acts, we read of Paul or Peter preaching and conversions taking place. We have only summary statements, so we don't know everything that turned the hearers into eager converts. Sometimes miracles of healing drew them, but probably not always. In the hostile culture in which they lived, it certainly had to be more than words.

We have the Bible, which is God's Word, and that gives us the information we need to begin the faith journey and to live it. But for others to become serious believers takes more than merely proclaiming to them what God says. It also involves the messenger being a credible example of godliness.

In the above story, I wanted to show the initial fear of an African boy melting as the white-skinned stranger demonstrated his faith by his kindness, which was reflected in his face. As Proverbs 15:13 says, "A happy heart makes the face cheerful."

## About the Author

**Cecil Murphey,** whose books have been on the *New York Times* best-seller lists, lived in Kenya for six years. He is the author or coauthor of more than 135 books, including *90 Minutes in Heaven* with Don Piper, *Gifted Hands: The Ben Carson Story,* and *I Believe in Healing* with Twila Belk.

# 6

# Rag Doll

## by Kathy Ide

Really, Mom?" Megan raised an eyebrow at the picture her mother had cut out of a magazine. The little girl with dark brown braids held a Raggedy Ann doll like it was her most treasured possession, despite the marker scribbles on its cloth legs and the frazzled red yarn on its head. "This is how you see me?"

Her mom beamed as she ran a glue stick along the back of the picture. "Don't you remember? I made you a doll just like that. You took it everywhere. No matter how ratty it looked, you loved it with all your heart."

The other guests at Megan's bridal shower heaved a collective "Awwww." So into the collage it went, along with cutouts of wedding rings, waterfalls, pizza, chocolate, and other things her friends had found that reminded them of special memories they shared.

Megan's maid of honor placed a glass square over the hodgepodge of pictures, twisted the metal tongs on the back, then presented Megan with the gift, to the delighted squeals of her friends.

The opening notes to "Here Comes the Bride" rang from Megan's purse. "Sorry. I know the guest of honor shouldn't take a call in the middle of her own party, but—"

They all urged her to answer, knowing she'd set that ring tone exclusively for Patrick.

While the hostess directed everyone toward the cake table, Megan ducked into the hall for privacy. "Hey, lover," she cooed into the phone.

"Miss York?"

She started at the unfamiliar voice. "Yes," she choked out. "Who's this?"

"Do you know Patrick McKenna, ma'am?"

Her stomach knotted. Pat should be on a plane right now, headed for his old neighborhood. His best friend from high school had offered to throw him a bachelor party. Had someone found—or stolen—his cell phone?

"Ma'am?"

She cleared the lump in her throat. "He's my f-fiancé. How did you get his phone?"

"I'm sorry to have to tell you this, ma'am, but … Mr. McKenna's plane crashed."

The caller kept talking, but Megan didn't hear another word.

"No!" Megan glared at her parents, fists clenched around the brand-new white nightgown she would never wear. "I'm sick of your lies." She tossed the silky abomination into a black trash bag.

Her father reached for her, but she shrank from his touch. His misty eyes revealed a pain deeper than any she'd ever seen.

"Sweetheart." Mom wrung her hands. "We don't understand why this happened any more than you do. Sometimes God's ways are—"

"Stop it!" Megan's rapid breaths and shaky legs nearly caused her to collapse, but angry determination kept her standing. "I told you, I don't want to hear another word about God. Ever."

Turning away from her parents' grief-stricken faces, she went back to stuffing marriage-related items into large plastic bags and personal possessions into a suitcase.

How many years had she wasted following the God her parents believed in? Her entire life they'd filled her brain with stories about a loving heavenly Father. One who sent His Son to live a perfect, sinless life on earth. And how Jesus intentionally let people mock, torture, and finally kill him in the most inhumane way known to mankind. All to pay the penalty for the sins of every human who ever lived. So the Holy Spirit could dwell in their hearts, bring them joy on earth, and give them eternal life in heaven, where there would be no pain, no sorrow, no … death.

*Stupid fairy tale.*

She'd willingly swallowed the propaganda spoon-fed to

her by a long line of Sunday school teachers, pastors, and youth leaders. She and Patrick met on a mission trip to Oaxaca. Dated for two years—most of their "dates" being Bible studies and prayer meetings. When Pat proposed, he said he knew their marriage was God's will.

Like a blind fool, she'd shouted, "Yes!" and leapt into his arms, convinced the Creator of heaven and earth had handpicked him for her.

*So much for divine direction.*

Megan pulled on the zipper of her overstuffed suitcase. When it caught on a corner, she nearly collapsed in frustration. As she yanked to free it, old patterns of thinking kicked in. Was this setback God's way of trying to get her to reconsider her plan? Mentally tossing that crazy idea into the nearest trash bag, she unzipped an inch or two, freed the T-shirt sleeve that had gotten caught in the metal teeth, then closed the suitcase.

"Are you sure you won't change your mind?" Dad's normally polished pastor's voice sounded gravelly and strained. "Carmen and Jeanne would love to have you stay with them for a while."

Megan tugged the bulging suitcase off the bed. She loved her aunt and uncle. But they'd only give her more of the same dog-and-pony show she'd been duped with her whole life. It was time to grow up.

"I'll call when I get to LA." Everyone in her little Illinois hometown considered California "the land of fruits and nuts," and Los Angeles the moral armpit of the world. What better place to get as far away from religious fanaticism as possible?

When Megan reached her bedroom doorway, Mom stepped into her path, holding out Megan's study Bible. "At least take this with you."

For years that book had been her most valued possession. She'd read it from cover to cover, multiple times. So many pages were dog-eared, verses underlined, and passages highlighted, it looked as tattered as the Raggedy Ann in her bridal collage.

Megan's eyes cut to the shattered glass and ripped paper in the corner of her room. She'd made a mess of the gift her family and friends had lovingly put together for her. But the God she'd always believed in had made a mess of her life. Seemed only fair.

Gazing at the Book in her mother's hands, Megan whispered, "Sorry, Mom." Then left the room.

"We'll be praying for you," her parents called after her.

*Go ahead. Knock yourselves out.* Never again would she speak to a God who, if He even existed, would lead her into supreme bliss, only to steal it away in such a cruel, heartless manner. Especially after she'd given her whole life to Him.

"Hey, chubby, where's that coffee I asked for—twice?"

Megan bit back the retort that came to mind. She couldn't risk losing her job at this cheesy dive. It didn't pay squat, but it came with insurance. If she got fired, no new employer would cover her "preexisting condition."

She pasted on a half-smile as she poured the nasty-smelling brew. "Sorry for the wait. Can I get you anything else, sir?" She hoped he didn't notice the sarcasm she couldn't keep out of her tone.

"Just the check."

After handing him the bill, she headed back to the kitchen, rubbing the small of her back. There were days when she wished she'd taken her girlfriends up on their offer to pay for an abortion.

A grip on her forearm stopped her. "What does this say?" Her boss waved an order slip in her face.

"Ham-and-cheese omelet, hold the peppers."

"Well, that's not what the lady at table six got. And she says you never came back to check on her, so she couldn't correct the order."

Megan sighed. "I'll go talk to her."

"Too late," he growled. "She just stormed out of here, after chewing me out … without paying her bill."

"Sorry."

"So am I." He handed her an envelope. "I took the cost of her meal out of your last paycheck."

"Hank, please—"

"Don't argue. This isn't the first time you've messed up. Turn in your apron. And don't ever come back."

Megan woke up slowly, head pounding, unable to open her eyes. When she tried to roll over, her right arm felt as if it were tied to something. She forced her lids to raise a bit. Through tiny slits, she saw bright lights and a room full of white. Was that smell … disinfectant?

"She's coming around." An excited voice. Vaguely familiar.

"M-m-mom?" The word came out weak and thready.

A warm hand grasped hers. "I'm here, sweetie. So's Dad." Sniffling.

A spasm of shivers overtook her. Megan felt like she'd been poured into a blender on high speed. Her entire body went into convulsions. "Oh, God, help me!"

The pain became unbearable. Mercifully, she lost consciousness.

Megan gazed in her bedroom mirror at the reflection of her stomach—flat, except for a small mound of residual "baby fat." Her heart clenched.

She hadn't wanted to bring a child into her lousy world. But she'd looked forward to giving her baby to a loving couple who wanted to adopt. In her attempt to end her own life with an overdose of pills, she'd stopped another beating heart … and deprived a family of a child they desperately longed for.

With a soft knock on the open door, her father entered. "How are you feeling, honey?"

"Okay." Physically, anyway. Emotionally, she wasn't sure she'd ever recover.

If she did, her parents would get the credit. They'd flown

in the day she was rushed to the hospital, and one or both of them had been at her bedside 24/7. After she was released, they'd brought her home. They took care of her, even when she went through dramatic mood swings, severe anger, and clinical depression.

"Why have you and Mom been so patient with me?" Megan asked. "I've given you nothing but grief since the day I left."

He wrapped strong arms around her trembling frame. "You're our daughter. We'll always love you, no matter what."

Megan's throat closed up. As she melted into Dad's embrace, she sensed God saying the same thing to her heart. In spite of everything, she was His child. And He loved her … unconditionally.

Over her father's shoulder, Megan gazed at the collage on the wall. Behind a new pane of glass were all the pictures from her bridal shower. In the center, a smiling girl in braids held a ratty-looking doll—scuffed, worn, bedraggled. But completely and purely loved.

## Life Application

When bad things happen, we may question God's love, His sovereignty, even His existence. But like a loving earthly father, whose heart never changes—even when his little girl tries to run away from home, or his teenage son hollers, "I hate you," or his grown children decide they don't need him anymore—God continues to love us.

Though His heart grieves when His children turn away from Him, His love never changes. His grace is not dependent on our actions, thoughts, or feelings.

Some people think they're too messed up for God to love them. Others are so confident in their self-achieved morality, they don't believe they need God. But our heavenly Father loves all His children equally—no matter how bad, or good, they are.

In spite of what you've done or what you've thought about God—even if you've denied His existence—He is waiting, with open arms and a forgiving heart, to welcome you home and fill your life with joy and peace that surpass circumstances.

### About the Author

**Kathy Ide,** author of *Proofreading Secrets of Best-Selling Authors,* is a freelance editor/mentor for new writers, established authors, and book publishers. She speaks at writers' conferences across the country. She is the founder and director of The Christian PEN and the Christian Editor Connection. For more, visit KathyIde.com.

# 7

# Prairie Lessons

## by Deborah Raney

*J*shooed away the dogs and carried my breakfast out to the back deck. It was a tradition Grant and I had shared for most of our married life, and I'd just recently been able to enjoy the deck again without it bringing back too many difficult memories.

I placed my bagel and steaming coffee mug on the wobbly table and stepped to the rail. The April air was cool, but the bright sun climbing over the hedgerow at the edge of the farm promised to warm things up in a hurry. The sapphire skies of that Kansas morning, and the greening wheat fields that rolled across the prairie, should have filled me with hope.

But hope had been a stranger to me for longer than I cared to admit.

While Buster and Lad trotted off to the barn, King, our old collie, came to the rail beside me, cocking her head, watching to see if I would allow her to stay. She must have been close to a hundred in dog years, and she walked with an arthritic limp. Like a half dozen other lucky dogs over the years, she'd been dumped off in our yard when the boys were small, and they had named her King before they realized she was female.

King pressed her wet nose in the palm of my hand and whimpered. I knew how she felt. We'd both been abandoned. First by three boys off to college in quick succession, and then by Grant who, as far as King was concerned, had been just another overgrown boy.

King was the one who'd discovered Grant in the barn that awful morning. I wondered if dogs remembered things the way people did. For her sake, I hoped not. The vision of my husband's crumpled form at the foot of the hayloft ladder still haunted me.

After the funeral, Eric had offered to quit his job, and Jon and Mitch both agreed to leave college and come home to keep the farm running. But I couldn't ask them to do that. The farm wasn't our entire livelihood. The economy had long ago dictated that Grant take a full-time job in town. His hours at the lumberyard had paid the bills, which allowed us to stay on the farm. His life insurance had left me in decent shape financially.

The smart thing would be to sell the farm, but I knew that would never fly with my sons. They loved this place. It was the only home they'd ever known, the only thing they had left of Grant.

I loved it, too, for that matter. I couldn't imagine ever leaving, but neither did I see how I could possibly keep the place up by myself. The boys helped when they were home, but three or four weekends a year just wouldn't cut it.

King barked at a small cloud of dust half a mile or so up the dirt road. It was too small to be a car, and as the dust rolled closer I realized what—or rather *who*—it was. I grumbled under my breath and seriously considered whisking my breakfast inside and pretending not to be home.

I ripped off a bite of my soggy bagel and chewed furiously. My stomach had turned sour by the time I heard the annoyingly familiar sound of the rusty old bicycle chain clanging against its even rustier frame.

King limped off the porch and greeted Robert J. Simmons with a wagging tail and a friendly bark. *Traitor*, I thought, glaring at King. But for Mitch's sake, and for Grant's, I forced myself to be civil.

"Good morning, Robert."

"Mornin', Miz Keene," he muttered, gazing lazily at the sky. "Nice day, huh?"

*Well, it was*, I thought, draining my coffee mug. *Before you showed up.*

"Mitch was just home last weekend," I informed Robert. "He probably won't be back till school's out."

"Yeah, he told me that." Robert stood at the bottom of the deck steps, rubbing King's head with one hand and holding up his bicycle with the other. The hem of his jeans ended just above the tops of his striped athletic socks. His eyeglasses were smudged, and the earpiece on one side had been mended with black electrical tape. Dark greasy hair curled over his ears.

Mitch had befriended Robert when they were in junior high. Robert wasn't exactly retarded, but he wasn't the brightest bulb in the marquee either. *Socially retarded* was probably the most accurate description.

Grant and I had been proud of the way our youngest son stood up for this social misfit against the other kids' cruelty. Mitch had endured Robert's undying loyalty ever since.

After Mitch went off to college, Grant took Robert under his wing, allowing him to tag along while he did farm chores or worked on the old Chevy truck that was Grant's pride and joy.

"The kid's not as dumb as you'd think, Annie," Grant had told me more than once. "He's got a good mechanical mind. Shame he doesn't have much chance to put it to use." I'd drawn the line when Grant tried to get Robert involved on a repair job inside the house.

I hadn't counted on Robert's loyalty transferring to me once Grant was gone and Mitch headed back to college. It was not an inheritance I relished.

Robert stood, head down, still patting King and holding up his bike. After three interminable minutes I picked up my breakfast dishes, hoping he'd take the hint. He didn't.

I went into the kitchen and put my dishes in the sink to soak. When I came back out, Robert hadn't budged. I couldn't bring myself to kick him off the farm, but I had several projects lined up and I was determined not to let him spoil my day.

I started toward the barn, where I was planning to make

a plant stand for the deck. Grant had purchased the kit from a mail-order catalog, apparently a surprise for my birthday. UPS had delivered it two weeks after he died.

Though I'd never been handy with tools, I was determined to put this thing together if it killed me. And it just might. The blurb in the catalog promised "easy assembly," but the instructions that came with the kit might as well have been in Swahili. It had taken weeks to psyche myself up for the task, but I'd actually been looking forward to it. Until Robert showed up

I strolled past him without speaking, but my jaw tightened when I heard him lean his bike against the deck and follow me. King trotted after both of us, panting happily. I glanced over my shoulder and saw that she was smiling in the peculiar way of collies.

I opened the big sliding door at the end of the barn and wrestled an oversized slab of plywood onto two sawhorses. Robert stood and watched while I took the boards from the packing box and smoothed out the instructions on my makeshift table. After I stared at them for several minutes, I began to see how these ten boards could eventually become the attractive display piece pictured in the catalog.

Following the instructions, I anchored the bottom slat between the two boards that would form the sides of the shelves. I found the Phillips-head screwdriver in Grant's toolbox and set to work.

Robert sniffed and wiped his nose on the back of his hand. "You want some help?"

"No, Robert," I replied, more curtly than I'd intended.

"I could hold the boards for you."

"No, thank you," I repeated firmly. "I'm kind of looking forward to doing this on my own. It was a gift from Grant … for my birthday." I teared up unexpectedly and wondered why I felt I owed this intruder an explanation.

"Oh," Robert grunted.

After five minutes of blister-raising effort, I was still turning the first screw, and it still protruded from the wood a good half inch. *If that idiot wasn't standing here watching every move I make …* I kept turning the screwdriver, the resistance growing stronger with every twist of my wrist.

"Surprised it ain't countersunk," Robert mumbled.

"Huh?"

"Surprised it ain't countersunk," he repeated in the same monotone. He picked up a small plastic packet of wood plugs from the pile of screws lined up on the worktable. "Usually if they give you these plugs, the screws are countersunk."

I laid down the screwdriver and wiped the sweat off my forehead with the tail of my T-shirt.

Robert took a hesitant step forward. "I could turn it for a while. I'm pretty strong."

I seethed at the interruption, though my conscience had begun to prick.

"You want me to turn it for a while?"

"No, Robert, I don't." I felt bad for the way the words came out, especially when I saw him slink back a few steps.

I continued putting in screws, turning till I couldn't turn

anymore, bad-mouthing the imbecile who'd packed screws in this kit that were half an inch too long.

Robert watched in silence, but I could tell by the way his hands twitched that he was dying to get hold of my screwdriver.

I was being selfish. I knew that. I felt sorry for the kid. I truly did. The oldest of six children of an alcoholic father and a worn-down mother, Robert had a rough life. *But Lord*, I prayed, *he's not my problem. And in case You hadn't noticed, I've had it a little rough lately myself.*

I pretended to pore over the instructions, but in truth I was praying … and confessing. *Forgive me.*

I heard the Lord's reply loud and clear. *Robert needs to help you, Annie.*

I got the message. I had much to be thankful for. This boy needed to be needed. Surely that was the least I could do for him.

"You thirsty, Robert?"

He nodded.

I held out the screwdriver. "Tell you what. You work with these screws for a minute and I'll go make us some lemonade." I could always undo the damage later.

When I returned to the barn bearing two icy glasses of lemonade and a much-improved attitude, Robert was beaming. "Turns out they *was* countersunk, Miz Keene," he crowed. "You had both them boards on there backwards! See? But don't worry. I fixed it."

I examined the beginnings of my plant stand and saw that

each screw was neatly sunk into a hole drilled just for that purpose, leaving an indentation that would be covered by the wood plugs provided in the plastic packet. *So much for idiots and imbeciles.*

That's when it hit me. I'd heard the Lord's voice all wrong. He hadn't said, *Robert needs to help you.* He'd said, *You need Robert's help.*

My throat tightened, and I wanted to fall to my knees in humility … or on my face in humiliation. *I'm so sorry, Lord.*

Figuring that a display of repentance might embarrass Robert, I simply said, "Well, I'll be! You're right. I should've let you have a go at it a long time ago."

His ear-to-ear grin assured me I'd been forgiven.

While I sipped lemonade in the shade, Robert built me the sturdiest plant stand I've ever owned. It sits out on the back deck to this day. Sometimes, when he's not too busy with the farm chores, Robert helps me water the colorful geraniums and begonias that spill over the edges of its shelves.

I have a sneaking suspicion that Grant is smiling in heaven, knowing that his last gift to me taught me the real truth of that old adage "It is more blessed to *receive* than to *give.*"

## Life Application

Sometimes the difficulties of life weigh us down, and doing nice things for others feels like a burden.

Pride creeps in if we think our good works happen in

our own power. Reminding the first-century believers of the words in Proverbs, Peter said, "All of you, clothe yourselves with humility toward one another, because, 'God opposes the proud but gives grace to the humble.' Humble yourselves, therefore, under God's mighty hand, that he may lift you up in due time" (1 Peter 5:5–6). When we are truly yielded to Him, ministering by His power alone, we begin to see ourselves as we really are: redeemed slaves rather than godly saints.

God often places us in situations where we are on the receiving end of someone's kindness. This is a humbling experience, especially when we are accustomed to ministering to others. But when we let people serve us, we give them the chance to serve God as well.

God knows our human frailties and has already forgiven them. When we belong to Him, because of Christ's shed blood, God sees only righteousness when He looks at us. Only rightness before Him allows us to minister and be ministered to with the same gracious spirit.

## About the Author

**Deborah Raney's** first novel, *A Vow to Cherish*, inspired the film of the same title and launched Deb's writing career. Twenty years, thirty books, and numerous awards later, she's still writing. She and her husband, Ken, live in Kansas and have four grown children and five grandchildren who all live much too far away. Visit Deb on the web at DeborahRaney.com.

# 8

# The Pain Redemption

by Roxanne Anderson

This is going to be more painful than you could ever imagine."

Jesus turned from where he had been sitting at his Father's feet and looked up at his face. He thoughtfully considered his Dad's words as his mind went into the future. "Yes. That flogging and crucifixion will certainly test my physical limits in human form." He glanced down at his perfect palms, flipped them over and back, and imagined them punctured with rough nails. "But if that is your plan, I will manage to endure it."

The Father put his hand on his son's shoulder and looked intently into his eyes. "I am not speaking of the crucifixion."

"What then?"

"The greatest pain your brothers and sisters on Earth experience is not physical."

Jesus directed his thoughts to the past, his omnipotent

consciousness turning deliberately though the pages of mankind's history. A history he had fully participated in.

As his perfect memory flowed into a tributary of eternity, he thought of all the different kinds of pain the first sin had brought into their perfect creation. A flood of carnage, deterioration, sickness, and perversion had been released when their best friends, Adam and Eve, exchanged sweet, divine friendship for a carnal, saccharine lie. That one sin started a downward spiral that had spun deeper and deeper into a cesspool of darkness and evil that now affected every life form, from its beginning until its death. That inevitable death was the ultimate price of sin, owed by everyone and everything on the beautiful planet they had formed out of nothing.

Jesus remembered how devastated he had been when Adam traded away their daily companionship like so much garbage. He had been shocked to see Adam not only turn on them, but also lash out against their friend Eve, Adam's soul mate and lover, designed specifically for him … and then try to blame her for his mistake. She in turn blamed the deceiver.

With their mutual trust and respect destroyed, those two were at odds for the rest of their days. That betrayal begat more betrayal, and a few years later, Adam and Eve's son tricked and murdered his younger brother out of jealousy. Their descendants carried on the tradition until the present day, when it seemed everyone on Earth could go from so-called love to hate in a human heartbeat.

And then he knew. Jesus' eyes met those of his Father. "Is

it …?" He swallowed. Was he really expected to become a target of the worst of human hatred, backstabbing, and betrayal?

"Yes."

"And is that emotional pain truly worse for them than for us?"

The Father removed his hand from Jesus' shoulder and sat back on his throne. He looked out beyond Jesus, his eyes reflecting the distant galaxies. "From my perspective, yes. Unlike us, they cannot live or feel in any time but the present. When they are hurt, their emotions, in the present-tense dimension, consume their bodies and their minds. This pain fills their tiny internal reality, making it a suffocating prison. Many never escape from it."

Jesus tried to comprehend a time-limited, individual human comprehension of pain, of feeling hurt and betrayed without knowing the future or perceiving all the circumstances. He attempted to funnel his omniscience into a diminutive theoretical reality of not knowing all. He shook his head with the effort.

The Father returned his gaze to Jesus and looked at him steadily. "But my perspective from here is objective. You will have the opportunity to find out firsthand what human pain truly feels like."

"Am I to experience every kind of emotional pain?" Jesus drew back, pondering what life might feel like in a mortal body with its fragile human psyche.

"You know the prophesies we gave to Isaiah, telling of your rejection by Israel."

"Of course. But I hadn't fully considered how that rejection would feel coming from individual people."

The Father winced almost imperceptibly, and his hands tightened on the arms of his throne. "You will be questioned by siblings who share your human mother and grow up with you. You will be doubted by neighbors who greeted you and ruffled your hair every morning of your childhood and adolescence."

Jesus was quiet for many measures, considering how many possibilities there would be to be hurt by people during thirty-three years of human life on Earth.

The Father's eyes shifted from Jesus to the stars. "And you will have a deserter and a betrayer in your inner circle of friends."

Jesus drew a sharp breath, remembering the pain of Adam's betrayal and how deeply it cut him, even in his divine state. He could still feel the ache of that loss, hundreds of human years later.

"Will I know which ones?"

The Father deliberately relaxed his grip and took a deep breath. "As an adult, you will be omniscient in your knowledge, yet still have to function daily within the limits of your human mind. In the fullness of time, when you begin your official season of ministry, you will know the weak and evil hearts of all men and women. Yet you will still give your friendship to them." He smiled wistfully. "The same way we do now, as much as we can with them in their fallen state."

"Only their rejection will hurt me more while I am a human." Jesus' statement hung as a question.

"Definitely." There was no hesitation in the finality with which his Father answered.

Jesus put his head in his hands and closed his eyes. "Is feeling all that emotional pain absolutely necessary?" He knew the answer, but desired to hear it from his Father's lips.

His Dad leaned forward. "Your primary mission is to show them how much we miss them, and the fellowship we had in the garden, the fellowship they were created for. You will demonstrate our obsession for personal relationships by choosing friends. You will share good times and bad with them. Laugh together, cry together, eat together, be hungry and tired together. You will worship me with them, pray to me with them, serve me with them. You will share our secrets with them. You will show them everything good that has ever been in our hearts for them from the beginning, which is now being restored through you, the perfect sacrifice. They will all pledge their loyalty and lifetime friendship to one another and to you."

"Yet in spite of all this, some of these closest friends will hurt me." Jesus spoke without looking up.

The Father rested his hand gently on Jesus' head. "Some will simply let you down. Many will leave you. Some will turn against you. Still others will lie and deny they ever knew you. And one …"

Jesus deliberately turned his thoughts away from visualizing the man of whom his Father spoke. "And I will have to treat him just like all the others."

"Yes. You will fully bear the pain of his betrayal, as one

of your dearest companions. You will also know what it feels like to have family members, friends, and trusted religious leaders who are supposed to be representing me talk about you behind your back, insult you to your face, lie to you and about you."

Jesus could almost feel the burning ache of it now. "Why? Why must I go through all that?"

"So that you will understand them, and the effects of sin on their lives, far more intimately than we do now."

This truth rang deeply into Jesus' being. The essence of the heart and soul he shared with the Father was to know and be known, to love and be loved. He sat up and leaned back against his Dad to be nearer to him … while he still could.

"After the fulfillment of all the prophesies, after your resurrection and return home, when your brothers and sisters who are left on Earth cry out to you in the throes of their anguish after being cheated on, lied to, lied about, turned on, turned out, and turned against, you will be the Savior and the High Priest who comprehends their agony firsthand. You will not know it in theory, or from a safe, omnipotent distance, but having lived through it all as the Son of Man. Your previously human yet always perfectly holy heart will go out to them, and they will be comforted."

Jesus' consciousness moved from focusing on the coming pain to the eternal purpose. This was indeed their divine blueprint, a plan that had been made before most of creation knew there would ever be a need for it.

The Father's expression grew soft. "I love them so much. I

can't wait to have them back, as close friends, the way it used to be. And when they return to me, I will heal all their pain—spiritual, physical, and emotional." He put his hand under Jesus' chin and gazed deeply into his eyes. "That is why I am asking you to redeem them."

Strength and resolve flowed into Jesus as he met his Father's intimate expression of ultimate power and pure devotion. Yes. He *would* take their love to Earth, and show it to his brothers and sisters, and win them back. He would endure all the pain that accompanied the loving, and not turn away from any of it. He would drink the cup of human rejection to its dregs. It would be worth the price to get his friends back, to regain the glorious fellowship they had with Adam and Eve in the garden, and to experience that friendship with all who would accept it. He caught a glimpse of what that would be like in the eons to come, of all the amazing human friendships he would experience after the door to God's presence was flung open once again and redemption complete.

Jesus drew a deep breath and returned his Father's look of love, accepting the invitation written there. "When do I go?"

## Life Application

We don't know what transpired between the Father and the Son before Jesus came to Earth. No conversation like the above is recorded in the Bible. We also don't know what Jesus thought or felt before He came to Earth. But we do know, from what is recorded in the Gospels, that He experienced many emotions while He was here, including compassion, rejection, anger, and sadness … and most of all, love. His great love for us motivated Him to come to live as one of us and go through intense suffering on our behalf. His sacrifice provided for us to be redeemed from our sin and separation from God and to have a close relationship with Him.

Hebrews 4:15–16 (NLT) sums it up perfectly: "This High Priest of ours [Jesus] understands our weaknesses, for he faced all of the same testings we do, yet he did not sin. So let us come boldly to the throne of our gracious God. There we will receive his mercy, and we will find grace to help us when we need it most."

## About the Author

**Roxanne Anderson** lives in Dallas, Texas. Her life is passionately defined by parenting three teenagers, her work as a midwife, her experience and involvement with missions around the world, and with writing. She blogs, rather candidly, at RoxannesWildWorld.blogspot.com.

# 9

# The Guilty Party

by Nancy Arant Williams

Kaylie Gentry lit a match in the darkness and stared at it vacantly. It had nearly burned her fingers when she suddenly came back to earth and blew it out. The grill was still cold, and the plate of hamburgers sat waiting. A mosquito buzzed around her head. She swatted at it, sighed, and whispered, "Lord, what do I do with my secret?"

The sliding door opened behind her. "Anything wrong, honey?" Jeff asked. "Want me to start the grill?"

"Oh," she stuttered. "Uh … sure. Thanks."

In the moonlight that reflected off the ocean, she could see his kind, caring face. He took the box of matches from her hand and smiled, gently kissing her lips.

She didn't feel very lovable. When he turned to light the grill, she shook her head. How could two bad decisions still haunt every minute of her life?

Jeff lit the coals, transferred the hamburger patties from plate to grill, then looked at her with concern. "What's the matter?"

"Oh, nothing," she murmured.

The night was perfect, just what most honeymooners would have ordered. She should've been grateful for the beautiful bridal suite overlooking the moonlit beach and for her adoring groom. Five more days remained of what should be wedded bliss, but she could only hope to survive them. The first two days had been nerve-wracking.

Jeff took her in his arms. "Why won't you tell me what's wrong?"

"Nothing's wrong," she insisted gently. "I'm fine. Really. Just tired."

"Well, after we eat, you can lie down and rest." He kissed the tip of her nose and gave her a gentle smile. "Can't have my bride exhausted, now, can I?"

Once inside the hotel room, he pulled dishes out of the cupboard and set them on the counter, then pulled silverware from the drawer. "What would you like to drink? Wait, I know. Water, right?"

She nodded. She should be handling meal preparation, but her feet seemed to be made of lead, and for some reason a lump in her throat simply refused to budge.

"I'd better go turn the burgers. Don't forget me while I'm gone."

She smiled. What a silly thing to say. As long as she lived, she could never find anyone she loved as much as Jeff. He was everything she'd ever dreamed of in a man. She just couldn't understand what he saw in her.

Kaylie wandered into the living room, sank into the corner of the overstuffed loveseat, tucked her feet under her, and picked up the snapshots of their wedding. The pictures should have shown a rapturous bride gazing admiringly at her groom. Instead they showed a woman who felt unworthy of love.

Glancing at the balcony, she saw Jeff's back. Tears filled her eyes, but she brushed them away. No longer able to sit still, she strode to the bedroom and lay down. *What am I going to do, Lord?*

She glanced around, noticing for the first time her charming surroundings. The wallpaper was sea-foam green, pale blue, and tan, portraying a landscape of a beach with a swelling ocean tide, real enough that she could almost feel the spray on her face.

Kaylie frowned. She was sleepwalking through her life, her emotions buried deep, along with her secret. Its presence was poisoning her soul. But she couldn't figure out how to get rid of it or get past it.

Hearing the bedroom door slide open, she pulled herself to a sitting position and dried her cheeks.

"You hungry, sweetie?" Jeff asked.

"Not really."

He sat next to her on the bed and pulled her into his arms. "Kaylie, you know I love you, right?"

"Of course." She swallowed the tears that rose in her throat.

"And you trust me, right?"

"Yes, but—"

He cupped the back of her head and nestled it against his chest. "I don't know what's wrong, but I can tell something is eating you alive, and I think we need to talk about it." She heard a catch in his voice as he hugged her tightly. "Kaylie, I love you more than I ever thought I could love anyone. And I would do anything for you. But what you need most, I can't give, because I can't figure out what's wrong."

She sighed, wishing she had told him when he proposed, or even before. At least then he could've said good-bye before things got complicated. "What about your hamburgers?"

"You couldn't eat a bite right now, and neither could I." He caressed her cheek with the backs of his fingers.

Kaylie trembled for a moment, then sat up straight. "If I tell you, you'll hate me."

He pulled her into his arms. "I can't imagine anything you could've done that would make me want to leave."

She closed her eyes, hoping the words would come if she couldn't see his face while she said them. She took a long breath. "When I was seventeen, I fell in love with a guy I thought was a Christian. He said he loved me, and I trusted him. He said he wanted us to get married." Her voice shook as she brushed away tears.

Jeff handed her a handkerchief. She took it without looking up, staring at it as though talking to the white square of cloth.

"Even though I was a Christian, I let him make love to me. It was only once, but I ended up pregnant. I felt so bad I thought I'd die. When I told him about the baby, he laughed and said only stupid girls got pregnant. I never saw him again."

Jeff covered her hand with his and whispered, "Go on."

She had nothing to lose now. Might as well reveal the rest of the sordid details. "My parents and everyone at church thought I was a godly young woman, and I couldn't disappoint them. So I went to a clinic to get rid of my problem."

He tilted her face up to look into his eyes and held her chin in his hand. "You had an abortion?"

She bit her lip and studied his frowning face. "I knew it." She sobbed. "I knew you'd hate me if I told you."

He pulled her into his arms and held her close. "Honey, I don't hate you. It just doesn't sound like you. The tender-hearted Kaylie I know would never do something like that."

"Well, I did. I tried to change my mind when they put me on the table, but they strapped me down and I couldn't get away. I cried through the whole thing, knowing they were murdering my baby … and I had asked them to."

He gave her a tight squeeze. "Oh, sweetheart, you've been through something horrible, and you're still grieving. I've read that without help, it's nearly impossible to get over something like this."

She glanced up at him. "You don't hate me?"

"Of course not. You were barely out of childhood. You felt guilty and condemned, and you acted out of desperation. What you did was wrong, but it's forgivable."

"No, it's not," she whispered, barely able to speak for the sobs.

"Yes, it is." His voice was firm and confident. "There is no sin that God won't forgive if you ask Him."

"I've begged for forgiveness a million times. But I don't feel forgiven."

"Well, we're going to tear down that wall between us, and between you and God."

"How?"

"First, I'm going to pray."

She nodded, swiping at the waterfall of tears.

He stroked her back. "Lord, Kaylie and I need special grace right now. But I'm grateful that at least the truth is out. Help her to feel Your forgiveness and Your love. Break through the painful scar tissue and replace it with tender new skin, beautiful and sensitive. Restore what the canker has eaten, and heal her grieved spirit. I thank You, Lord, for Kaylie's gentle, gracious beauty, which so reflects Your heart. We stand against the Enemy, who would use her tender heart to condemn her. I trust, God, that You will finish the wonderful work you've begun in my darling bride. In Jesus' mighty name we pray and believe, amen."

Kaylie shyly glanced up at her wonderful husband. His handsome smile rained on her, soaking the arid ground of her soul. "You really don't hate me, do you?"

He chuckled. "If anything, I love you more, because I finally understand your pain." He kissed her forehead. "And from now on, I don't want anything to come between us, okay?"

She smiled freely for the first time in years. "I feel like I just dropped a thousand-pound weight off my chest."

"That's because you did."

Kaylie shook her head. "I don't know how you can be so understanding."

"Imperfect people identify with the flaws in others. I'm kind of glad to know you're just as vulnerable as I am."

With the tears finally over, Kaylie kissed his lips. And now, having nothing to hide, she knew she would fall in love with Jeff—and with God—more deeply than ever.

## Life Application

Do things from your past haunt you, stealing your victory and keeping you in turmoil? Are you afraid that people would love you less if they knew about them?

Psalm 32:3–5 states, "When I kept silent, my bones wasted away through my groaning all the day long. For day and night your hand was heavy on me; my strength was sapped as in the heat of summer. Then I acknowledged my sin to you and did not cover up my iniquity. I said, 'I will confess my transgressions to the Lord.' And you forgave the guilt of my sin."

Secrets have a way of becoming heavier the longer we carry them. And the Enemy's condemnation makes them even harder to bear. But most of the time, our fears of the consequences are worse punishment than anything anyone else could do to us.

When secrets are no longer hidden, they lose their power over us. We can safely dump our burdens at the foot of the cross. And as the light of God's Word shines into the darkness of our secret souls, the Enemy loses his power, and his threat is disarmed.

Our heavenly Father longs to set us free from condemnation and doubt. He wants to shatter the despair that keeps us bound, preventing us from living as children of the Most High God and heirs to the kingdom. But He can't help us until we are ready to admit what is wrong.

God made human beings to have a relationship with Him. When sin gets in the way, that relationship is broken, and pain results. And no matter how much we try to rationalize it, our spirits condemn secret sin.

Everywhere we look, we can see real-life examples of people trying to anesthetize their guilt, but there is only one remedy. With confession, forgiveness, and restoration, intimacy can be rebuilt with the ones we love. Including our ever-gracious heavenly Father.

## About the Author

**Nancy Arant Williams** is a multi-published author and book editor. She and her husband live in the heart of the beautiful wooded Missouri Ozarks, where they welcome guests to exit the rat race and rest at The Nestle Down Inn Bed & Breakfast. Her greatest desire is for people to realize how deeply God loves them. Check out her website at NancyArantWilliams.com or NestleDownInn.com.

# 10

# A House with Pillows

by Kathi Macias

Seven year-old Jenny loved the sound of her mother's humming. It was one of the few constants in her life, and it made her feel safe.

"Mommy, what's that song?"

Her mother stopped spreading the sleeping bag on the ground next to the drugstore wall, where the two of them spent the night whenever they were unable to get into a shelter. Jenny saw her mom smile, even in the near darkness of the late-autumn evening.

"Do you like that song, baby?"

She nodded. "It's one of my favorites."

"It's called 'Blessed Assurance.' It was written by a blind lady named Fanny Crosby."

Jenny's eyes widened. "She was blind?"

"That's right. And yet she did amazing things in her

lifetime." Mama's smile widened until her eyes crinkled. "Just like you will someday."

Jenny wasn't so sure about that. There was nothing amazing about her or her life. "I like it when you hum songs. But why don't you ever sing the words?"

Mama's forehead puckered. "You know I forget things, sweetheart. The tune is always there, but the words hide from me sometimes." She returned to her task of setting up their bed. "Come on, baby. Crawl inside the sleeping bag so you don't get cold." She glanced at the sky. "It doesn't look like it'll rain tonight, so we can thank God for that. You know how much it rains in Oregon." She bit her lower lip. "We are still in Oregon, aren't we?"

Jenny's heart squeezed. Her mother's forgetfulness was getting worse. "Yes, Mama. We're in Portland."

She released a deep breath. "Good. Now come on, into bed with you. Then I'll hum to you until you fall asleep."

Within moments, they were snuggled in together, warming each other as Jenny tried to get comfortable with just a thin layer of fabric between her and the cold, hard concrete.

Mama stopped humming. "You okay, baby?"

"I'm fine. It's just …" She hated to complain, especially when her mother couldn't do anything to solve the problem.

Mama lifted up on one elbow and gazed down at her. Even with a smudge of dirt on her face and her dark hair slipping out of its ponytail, Mama was still the most beautiful woman in the world. If only her mind worked right.

"What is it, Jenny? What's wrong?"

She sighed, knowing her mother wouldn't dismiss the issue without an answer. "Well … the ground is kinda hard. I just …" She took a deep breath. "I wish we had pillows," she blurted out. "Even just one to share."

Mama's eyes looked sad. "I used to have pillows when I was a little girl. I wish you did too."

"It's okay. We have each other, and that's all that matters, right?"

Mama nodded. "And we have God. The three of us are all we need." She folded her hands. "Let's pray and ask for a miracle."

Jenny wished she could count on God to answer. But lately she hadn't been so sure He was even listening. Jenny couldn't count all the times she and her mother had prayed for things—important things, like food and a place to stay, family or at least friends. If God hadn't answered those big prayers, what made Mama think He'd pay attention to a prayer for something as silly as a pillow?

Though it seemed pointless to Jenny, praying always made her mother feel better. So she closed her eyes as her mother lay down beside her, holding Jenny close.

"Dear God, we don't want to sound ungrateful. You've given us so much, and You've taken good care of us all this time. But You know how I'd really like for Jenny to have the kind of life I had when I was growing up. We don't need anything fancy, Lord, but … maybe just a house we could sleep in at night. And pillows, God, please—at least one for my sweet girl. I know that's a big prayer, but it's not too big for You."

She planted a kiss on top of Jenny's head. "Thank You, God. Amen."

Hot tears bit Jenny's eyes. It was one thing to pray for enough food for the day, but a house with pillows? She sighed. How would her mother take the disappointment when God didn't answer?

Jenny awoke early the next morning, still cradled against her mother's shoulder. Her nose was cold, and even with the first signs of a rising sun, she was certain it would be chilly outside of the sleeping bag. But they couldn't stay in their cocoon forever. She'd learned the importance of clearing out of their little spot before the drugstore opened for business and customers started showing up.

"Mama." She touched her mother's cheek, hating to waken her. "We need to get up. It's morning."

Her mom's eyelids fluttered open, then she sat up with a start. Her shoulders tensed, and her eyes darted back and forth before coming to rest on Jenny. When their gazes connected, her body relaxed and her lips spread into a welcoming smile.

"Good morning, sweet girl."

"Morning, Mama."

"We'd better get going if we want a good place in line for breakfast at the mission."

Jenny's stomach growled. Her mother was right. They

didn't want to get there late and miss out. Besides, today was Wednesday, the day the mission served breakfast burritos—Jenny's favorite.

They rolled up their sleeping bag and tied it to Mama's backpack. Jenny carried her own backpack, filled with two changes of clothes, three books, and one stuffed animal.

They showed up at the mission before the food ran out. As they headed for the counter, a woman's voice stopped them. "Mary Franklin, is that you?"

Jenny's mother jumped.

"I'm sorry, I didn't mean to startle you." The middle-aged woman with short graying hair, whom Jenny recognized as one of the mission workers, hurried up beside them. "I was hoping you'd stop by today." She lowered her voice. "There was a lady here yesterday, looking for you."

Mama gasped. Her eyes looked frightened.

"Her name is Karen Franklin." The woman's voice lowered even more, and Jenny had to strain to hear. "She said she's your mother."

Mama's body trembled. "My … mother?" she squeaked.

Jenny took her hand and held it tightly.

Why would Mama be afraid of her own mother? Jenny had never met her grandparents. Her mom never talked about them. But surely this was good news … wasn't it?

The mission lady nodded. "That's what she said. She even had a picture of you from high school. She told me she's been looking for you for months. She wanted to let you know that your father is sick and he wants to see you."

Tears glistened in Mama's eyes. "Daddy is … sick? He wants … to see me?"

"According to your mother, they both want to see you." She fished in her jacket pocket and pulled out a crumpled piece of paper. "She left her number. Would you like me to call her?"

The tears in Mama's eyes spilled onto her cheeks. "I don't know. I …"

"I want to see Grandma and Grandpa!" Jenny covered her mouth when her mother's gaze lowered to her.

"They haven't wanted to see us before."

Jenny's heart hip-hopped around her chest. "But they do now. Isn't that all that matters?"

Her mom wiped her cheeks with her sleeve. "You're right. Maybe God is answering our prayer." She turned back to the mission lady. "Yes," she said, her body no longer trembling. "Please call them."

Jenny hoped her mother was right. But if this wasn't an answer to their prayers, it could turn out to be the biggest disappointment they'd had yet.

Jenny had never felt such a soft mattress in all her life. She peeked across the room to the matching bed where her mother lay, her eyes closed.

Jenny looked up at Karen Franklin, who sat on the edge of the bed, tucking the blankets around her. "Is this really the bedroom where my mama slept when she was little?"

"Sure is." The pleasant lady with the salt-and-pepper hair glanced toward Mama and then looked back at Jenny. "And the bed your mama's in now was for her friends when they stayed over."

Jenny thought of all the pictures she'd seen of her mother earlier that day, as the three of them sat on the couch looking through photo albums. She also thought of the man she'd met briefly when they stopped by the hospital. He'd told her he would surely get better and come home soon, now that he knew he had three beautiful ladies waiting for him.

"Why didn't you want to see us before?" The question popped out before Jenny could stop it.

Grandma's cheeks reddened, but she smiled and stroked Jenny's hair. "Your grandpa and I were wrong, honey. When your mama told us she was going to have a baby, we …" She snuck another peek at Mama before continuing in a whisper. "Your grandpa and I had always hoped she'd be married when she told us that news, but she wasn't. We were hurt and scared for her, especially with her— "

She released a long sigh. "I'm afraid we didn't handle things very well. We had a big fight, and your mother left home. Somehow we lost touch with her. After a while, your grandpa didn't want to talk about it. It just hurt too much. But when he got sick …"

Grandma wiped away a tear. "We had to try to find your mama—and you. I started calling all the homeless shelters around town." She sighed. "It took a few days to find you. But here you are."

"Here we are," Jenny whispered, a warm glow spreading through her tummy.

Her grandmother looked at Mama with sad eyes. "Now we can take your mother to the doctor so he can give her medicine for her … memory problems."

Jenny was happy to hear that. Her mother had always told her she'd probably remember things better if she had the right medicine.

Grandma fluffed the pillow under Jenny's head. "Would you like an extra one, dear? We have plenty."

Plenty of pillows. Not just one that she and Mama had to share, though that would've been enough. "Oh, yes, please," Jenny said. "That would be really nice … Grandma."

Her grandmother hugged her, squeezing her tightly for several minutes. Then she left the room to get the extra pillows.

Though Mama's eyes were still closed, she began to hum. Jenny recognized the tune. It was "Blessed Assurance."

## Life Application

How many times do we pray for something, yet we don't really expect an answer because we think our request is too big for God? Or perhaps we believe we aren't important enough to warrant an answer.

Jesus addressed this faulty thinking when He spoke to His disciples about God's infinite mercy and unfailing love. He wanted them to understand that though God is holy and sovereign, the Creator of the universe and everything in it, He cares for the minutest details of our lives.

Jesus said that almighty God takes note if even one little sparrow falls. Sparrows were common then, as they are now—considered nearly worthless compared to rare or exotic birds. And yet Jesus described the scope of God's love for people by saying, "If God cares for even a common sparrow, how much more does He care for you?" (See Matthew 6:26.)

God may not answer our prayers as quickly or specifically as he did with Mary and Jenny. But His love for each of us is infinite and unconditional. And He longs to give us what's best for us, even more than we long to do so for our children.

If God loves even the tiny sparrow that falls to the ground, how much more does He care for us, who are made in His very image?

### About the Author

**Kathi Macias** is a multi-award-winning author who has written more than forty books. In 2011, she won the Author of the Year award from BooksandAuthors.net, and her novel *Red Ink* was the Golden Scrolls Novel of the Year and a Carol Award finalist. Her novel *Unexpected Christmas Hero* was named 2012 Book of the Year by BookandAuthors.net.

# 11

# Be Grateful in All Things

by Diane Simmons Dill

*Not again!* My heart sank as I yanked the plastic waste-basket out from under the kitchen sink and watched water drip from it onto the floor. My husband had tried to fix that leak more times than I could count. He'd put a bowl under the faulty pipe, but I'd forgotten to check it and it had overflowed. Again.

We needed a plumber. But that was way out of our budget.

I dropped to my knees and sopped up the mess with a towel. *God, You formed the whole world. Can't You do something about bringing us a little more income? Or at least show Ben how to fix this stupid leak?*

As usual, my prayer was met with silence.

I grabbed the bowl full of water, stood, and dumped it down the sink. Then I stretched my aching muscles and pressed my fist into the small of my back. My whole body felt like it had gone through the proverbial wringer. Probably just stress related. If we hadn't lost our health insurance when my husband got laid off, I would've made an appointment with the doctor weeks ago.

Ben straggled into the kitchen, dressed in his robe. "Hey, hon." He headed for the coffee pot. "So, what's the good news this morning?"

I glared at his back. "The sink is leaking … but that's not news, is it?"

If he caught the sarcasm in my voice, he didn't show it. He just kissed me on the cheek and promised to take a look at the pipes as soon as his favorite television show was over. Then he headed into the living room, coffee mug in hand.

*Oh, sure. You go watch TV while I spend all morning doing housework.*

Ben watched documentaries almost every morning before heading out to the unemployment office or job interviews. When he first got laid off, I tried to watch them with him. But it felt like a waste of time, and I had a ton of chores to do.

"Hey, Katy," he called out. "Why don't you come watch this program with me? It's about alligators in South America."

Was he kidding? Another show about alligators? "Honey, if I have to watch one more documentary, I think I might run screaming from the house." I was only half joking.

Ben poked his head into the kitchen. "Aw, come on, babe. Take a break."

I scrunched the towel in my hands like I was wringing someone's neck. Which I kinda felt like doing.

He put down his coffee and took me into his arms. "I

know you're worried about our finances. But everything's gonna be all right. We just have to keep the faith." Ben gave my nose a playful tap with his forefinger.

I knew he was trying to cheer me up. But at the moment I had no interest in being cheerful. I wanted to holler and throw things. And faith? Sorry, I was fresh out.

I pulled away from his embrace and finished wiping the counter.

"At least the tire didn't go flat again this week." He winked.

Ben seemed to be in a perpetual good mood, no matter how fast our lives were crumbling around us. I knew I should be grateful for the few things that *weren't* going wrong. But at the moment, all I wanted was a partner at my pity party.

With a sigh, Ben returned to the living room.

A pang of guilt shot through me. I knew God loved my husband and me and that He wanted whatever was best for us.

*I'm sorry for my negative attitude, Lord. I do have faith, and I know You won't forsake us.* The words sounded hollow. I knew I wasn't acting the least bit Christlike. But every time I turned around, there was another leak, another flat tire, another *something.* When would it end?

I had to get out of this gloomy place, with irritating chores staring at me from every corner. After tossing the towel onto the washing machine, I headed for the coat rack by the front door. "I'm going for a walk. Maybe it'll clear my head."

"Okay, hon," Ben called without looking up from the television.

I grabbed my jacket to guard against the cool March air.

As I shut the door behind me, I fumbled with the zipper. *Great. I can't even get a stupid zipper to work right!*

Leaving my jacket open, I stomped down the steps.

At the edge of our front porch, I saw a daffodil thrusting its buttery yellow head toward the sun.

As I stared at the flower, my eyes misted. This tiny ray of sunshine stood alone in a patch of dry, barren dirt. Prickly weeds grew up all around it. A bitter-cold breeze wafted over it. Yet this lonely sentinel bravely heralded spring's imminent arrival.

A Bible verse I'd memorized long ago came to mind. "Consider the lilies of the field, how they grow: they neither toil nor spin; and yet I say to you that even Solomon in all his glory was not arrayed like one of these" (Matthew 6:28–29 NKJV).

Tears flowed as I thought of the shameful way I'd spoken to the Lord and to Ben. I had a lot to be grateful for. To begin with, I was alive on this cool but glorious March day, enjoying God's beautiful creation. I had a caring husband. We had a roof over our heads, clothes to wear, food to eat. And a God who really did love us.

But I'd been too busy feeling sorry for myself to notice my abundant blessings.

I knew what I had to do. Like that little daffodil reaching for the sun, I needed to reach for God's Son.

I sat on the cold wooden porch step. *I'm sorry, Lord. I've locked myself in a prison of unhappiness and ungratefulness. But I don't want to be there anymore. I want to feel joy and peace again.*

My heart felt a little lighter.

*Thank You, Lord, for every blessing You have so graciously showered upon me. You've been faithful to me even though I've acted like an immature child throwing a temper tantrum because everything wasn't going the way I thought it should.*

I stood and scurried back into the house with a spring in my step. I couldn't wait to throw my arms around my husband. "Ben! You have to come outside and see this magnificent daffodil I found."

He looked confused. "What are you talking about?"

"Just come with me." I took his hand, led him outside, and showed him God's spectacular handiwork.

Our financial worries hadn't disappeared. But if God could create such a lovely flower in the midst of bare dirt and weeds, He was more than able to provide for us. And He *would* provide, just as He promised in His Word. I didn't have to let worry or fear or doubts destroy my joy and peace. I just needed to be grateful for what I already had. The future was secure in the strong hands of the Lord. And spring was just around the corner.

As joy returned to my barren soul, I realized that God would show us His will … if I let go of my will first. And He would lead Ben to the right job or find some other way for us to manage.

Maybe He would even fix that leak!

## Life Application

The Bible tells us that we are to be grateful in all things. (See 1 Thessalonians 5:18.) But how is that possible when seemingly insurmountable obstacles sometimes block our paths?

One way to avoid worrying is to be grateful. I don't mean saying "thank you" when someone gives you a gift, although that's good. I'm talking about being truly grateful, even when things aren't going the way we think they should. No matter what our circumstances, we can always thank God for His grace and unconditional love.

Why do we hang on to our worries and refuse to let go? Maybe because we've tried placing trust in God in the past and couldn't manage to do it. But it's not impossible. We are capable of doing whatever the Lord commands, in His strength. (See Matthew 19:26; Philippians 4:13.)

As long as we are on this planet, we will have troubles. (See Job 14:1.) But we can decide how we react to them. We can choose to be content and grateful.

The next time something happens that appears negative, stop and talk to God about it. Let Him handle your burdens, and trust Him to provide. The result will be peace and joy, even if it doesn't come in the form you expect or in your timing.

Proverbs 7:3 urges us to write the words of the Lord on our hearts. One way to do that is to jot down Scripture verses on sticky notes and place them around the house, at work, or in the car. Then, when troubles crop up, the Holy Spirit will bring just the right passages to mind.

God's thoughts are not our thoughts, nor His ways our ways. (See Isaiah 55:8.) For that alone, if nothing else, we can be truly grateful.

## About the Author

**Diane Simmons Dill** graduated from the University of Alabama at Birmingham with a BA in creative writing and a minor in graphic design. She served as president of the SonShine Writers Group from June 2012 through December 2014. She lives in Alabama with her husband, Wayne, and their two spoiled cats, Maddie and Abby. Diane offers editing, publishing, and writing services. Visit her at Facebook.com/RightWriteProductions.

# 12

# A Waffle Stop Story of Love and Pistols

## by Buck Storm

Hey, Jess, you get lost back there? I'm dry!"

Jess rubbed her temples and glanced through the diamond-shaped window in the swinging door that separated the kitchen from the dining room. Seated at the counter, Harley Price wore a dirty white T-shirt with the slogan "I'm Old—Where's My Stinking Discount?" stretched over his gut. Seeing Jess, he held up his empty coffee cup and let it swing on one finger.

Jess didn't bother opening the door. "Relax, Harley. I gotta brew a new pot."

He grunted and waved her off with a fat hand, then stood and waddled away.

Breakfast special—sent back twice—nine cups of coffee, and no tip. *Ladies and gentlemen, Harley Price has finally left the building.*

Jess waited till he'd exited the front door of the Waffle Stop before grabbing the coffee pot and shouldering open the door.

The only remaining customer sat at the counter. She'd been there for more than two hours without ordering anything besides coffee.

Jess held up the pot. "Warm you up?"

The girl scratched at her head. Her black hair stayed standing where she'd rubbed, and dandruff peppered the shoulders of her tattered thrift-store pea coat. "Thought you had to brew fresh."

Jess winked. "I lied."

"Sure." As the girl pushed her cup toward Jess, her coat fell open a bit. Tiny blue veins road-mapped her collarbones and throat above a stained tank top. Nails ringed with dirt, her fingers trembled as she stirred in eight packets of sugar.

"Sweet tooth?" Jess said.

"Don't you have tables to wait on?"

"Nope. Breakfast rush is over." She waved her free hand over the empty diner. "Folks who want brunch or something fancy like that sure as heck don't come to the Waffle Stop."

"Yeah, well, I don't need anything."

"You don't want something to eat?"

"I said I don't need anything."

Vertical lines formed between the girl's eyes, and her hand moved into the folds of her pea coat. It stopped when the front door opened and a tinny electronic chime sounded.

A man ducked slightly as he entered, an inch or two of space separating his shock of gray hair from the doorjamb.

His dark, colorless suit, shiny at the elbows and knees, hung loose on his frame.

"Hey, Pop," Jess called out, grateful for his interruption of the tension in the room.

"Howdy, Jess." A few strides carried him across the café, and he took the stool next to the girl.

She glared at him. "You got a problem?"

A twinkle sparked in Pop's pale blue eyes. "Probably more than one. Try not to think about them if I can help it."

"This whole place is empty. Why do you have to sit next to me?"

"This is my stool. I always sit here. Good thing you weren't on it. I might've sat on your lap."

The girl curled her lip. "You some sort of freak?"

Jess pulled a mug from beneath the counter and poured. "How you feeling today, Pop?"

He turned the mug slightly, aligning the handle exactly parallel to the counter edge. "Oh, you know, Jess. I'm feelin' old more than anything else."

"Ain't that the way it goes."

Jess grabbed a rag and began her daily post-breakfast wipe-down, but kept an eye on the reflection of the man and girl in the mirror behind the pastry display.

"You her dad?" the girl asked.

"Odds're against it."

"Then why'd she call you Pop?"

He pointed a bony finger at a paper nametag stuck to the front of his coat. Following white words that said *Hello, My*

*Name Is* in block print on a blue background, the word *Pop* was written in black felt-tip marker. "'Cause that's my name."

"You don't have any other name?"

"Don't need any other."

Pop reached into his jacket pocket and pulled out three spoons. He placed them parallel to one another in a tight row six inches to the right of the coffee mug. Between the mug and spoons, he lined up three sugar packets, also evenly spaced, labels aligned and facing up.

"You bring your own spoons to a diner?"

"Don't you?"

"I knew it. You *are* a freak."

Pop shrugged. "I bring my own spoons, you bring your own *pistola*. We all got our little peccadilloes, don't we?"

At the word *pistola,* Jess's cleaning rag stopped and her pulse raced. She knew just enough Spanish to understand what that meant.

The girl gave Pop a long, hard stare. "Why'd you say I got a gun?"

"From the size of the barrel, I'm thinking it's about a forty-five. That old coat don't hide it too good. You could do with a new one. Coat, I mean. Not *pistola*."

*Stay calm and focus.* Jess glanced at the door to the kitchen. Could she make it before this crazy customer could pull out her weapon? Jess turned around slowly, ready to bolt.

The girl stabbed a finger at her. "You stay right where you are." Her hand went beneath the coat again and this time came up with a gun that might as well have been a cannon.

The girl's eyes widened as if she were as surprised as anyone at the weapon's sudden emergence.

She pointed the thing at Jess with a shaking hand. The quaver seemed to travel through her arm to her vocal chords. "I don't want no coffee. I don't want food. But I do want you to open the cash register and give me what's in it. Plus what's in that apron and any other cash you got around here. I wasn't gonna hurt nobody, but this old freak came in and might not leave me no choice. So you better just do it."

"I …" Jess's gut tightened. *Dear God, please make this end!* She didn't want to die in a Waffle Stop.

Pop tore the top off a sugar packet, poured its contents into his mug, and picked up the farthest spoon. He stirred exactly seven times, counting the rotations out loud. "You ever shoot anybody before?"

"Shut up."

"'Cause I have. And it ain't no three laps around the pony ride, I'll tell you that."

The girl swallowed. "You shot somebody? What, in the war?"

Pop wiped the spoon clean and returned it to his pocket. "Nope, in a bar. Sittin' on a stool. Just like you."

The girl's eyes widened. "You killed a guy?"

"Nah. I winged him good, but he pulled through. And I walked out with a whopping hundred and two dollars."

"You're a criminal?"

"Reformed, you might say. Least I hope so. That hundred and two dollars cost me fifty-seven years of my life. I've been out of the pen for a deuce last August."

"And now you're some kind of Good Samaritan? What'd you do, find Jesus in there?"

Pop smiled and tore open a second sugar. "More like He found me. Walked into my cell one night, sat down on the bunk just as calm as anything, and said, 'Pop, you and Me need to have us a little chat.' We been talkin' ever since."

"You really are a freak, you know that?"

"Maybe, maybe not." Pop stirred the sugar, exactly seven times, then wiped the second spoon and placed it in his coat pocket. "Jess, now, she's got herself a pretty little girl who's gonna be brokenhearted if her mama don't pick her up when school lets out in a few hours. Why would you want that?"

The image of her daughter's big brown eyes pressed into Jess's mind. What would Maddy do without her? *Please, God, get us all out of this alive!*

"Do I look like I care?" the girl snarled.

Pop studied her for a long moment. "Yeah. You do."

She shifted the gun from Jess and pointed the long, shaking barrel at Pop's face.

"Maybe I'll shoot you instead." The statement lacked the firm bones of conviction.

Pop gazed at her with sadness. "It'd be a better choice. Nobody'd miss an old con like me. Then again, you *could* just put the *pistola* down and let me buy you breakfast."

The girl squinted, but the gun came down a few inches. "Why would you buy me breakfast?"

"'Cause you're just like everyone else. Cons, preachers, presidents, waitresses—the uniform don't make no difference. We're all the same, deep down. We need somebody to give us a little love without asking for nothin' back. Ain't no mystery to it."

The gun lowered all the way to the counter, though the girl's knuckles were still white on the grip.

Jess released the breath she'd been holding. But she didn't dare move an inch.

"You don't know what I need," the girl sneered. "You don't know nothin' about me. A crazy old man like you can't even imagine the things I've done."

Pop raised a gray eyebrow. "I ain't always been old, ya know. But age don't matter. 'Sides, I ain't asking for your life history." He tore the third sugar and dumped in the contents. Seven turns of the third spoon … wipe … back to the pocket.

The girl watched the procedure. "My mom didn't come get me one day. You know, from school, like you said. I never saw her again." She stared at the counter for a few seconds, then slid the gun toward Jess. "Take it. It ain't loaded." A tear rolled down her acne-pocked cheek, and she wiped it with the heel of her hand.

Jess took the pistol and put it in a drawer under the counter, fighting tears of her own. Whether from relief or compassion, she couldn't tell. "Half the police department eats lunch here every day. I'll give it to one of them. Say somebody left it. No need to tell who."

The girl's shoulders relaxed a little and she nodded.

Pop handed the girl a menu and opened one of his own. "Well, will ya look at that. Ol' Waffle Stop is running a special. Free breakfast every day this week. Week after that too."

The girl swallowed a soft sob, but a smile broke through—her teeth brown and broken, the front two missing altogether. "Thank you … Pop."

He shrugged and took his first sip of coffee. "You're welcome, beautiful. You are surely welcome."

## Life Application

We are all far from beautiful. Yet somehow the Great Artist picks up our torn and tattered canvas and transforms us into what we were always intended to be—His masterpiece. What grace. What boundless, bottomless love.

We all sing in the choir of the broken. Imperfect. Lost. Wretched. God takes our sin and death and offers us—without cost—healing and life. How can we but follow our gracious Savior's example by allowing Him to embrace us with His perfect love?

### About the Author

**Buck Storm** has been blessed to see the planet with a guitar and a pocketful of stories. *The Miracle Man* (Lighthouse Publishing of the Carolinas/Heritage Beacon) is his first novel. Buck and his wife, Michelle, have a happy love story, a hideout in north Idaho, and two wonderful children.

# 13

# The Least of These

### by Dona Watson

laina got out of her Mustang and slung the straps of her business tote over her shoulder. Already the heat shimmered up from the blacktop in rippling waves. A lone bird chirped from the leafy jacaranda tree, its purple blossoms long gone. She stepped over the burger wrapper and the flattened paper cup in the gutter and onto a curb bordering a sketchy patch of dirt and yellow grass.

She double-checked the address on the folder in her hand, her eyes resting briefly on the little boy's name: Shaquis Jones. Now that he'd been with this foster family for a few days, it was time to check in. Alaina glanced at her watch and hoped this appointment would go quickly. She had four more cases to take care of before the day was through. Without looking back, she clicked the car door lock on her key fob—always a good idea in South Central Los Angeles.

She climbed three concrete steps up to the front door

and pressed the doorbell. A stuttered buzz inside was followed within seconds by approaching footsteps. The woman who opened the creaky door was probably near sixty, judging by the wrinkles in her smiling face. Perspiration dotted her ebony skin.

"Claire Johnson?"

"Mm-hm." Claire's voice purred like a mama cat's. "You must be Alaina." She twisted the lock on the metal screen door and pushed it open. "Come in, dear. It's hotter'n blue blazes out there."

Alaina thanked the woman and entered the dim living room, the shades drawn against the scorching heat outside. Stuffy and warm, the air smelled of bacon. Alaina wished she had taken the time to eat more for breakfast than a granola bar in the car.

"I imagine you'd like to see Shaquis?" Claire stood, hands clasped together as if she were a singer on stage.

Alaina nodded. "Yes, please."

Claire turned toward the hall. "Right this way, honey. He's playing in his room."

After a few steps down the short hallway, they reached an open bedroom door.

"Shaquis?" Claire's voice was gentle and kind. "There's a nice lady here to see you. Her name's Miss Alaina."

The six-year-old sat on the floor, rolling a Matchbox car along a road of gray plastic pieces snapped together to form an oval. Without pausing or looking up, Shaquis sputtered his lips together as he pushed the car down the narrow track.

Alaina nodded a thank-you to Claire and eased her way into the room.

She placed her purse and tote bag on the bed and sat cross-legged on the floor across from Shaquis, elbows on her knees. He wore blue jeans and a short-sleeved T-shirt, his feet clad in white socks. Black-and-blue bruises marred the skin of his thin brown arms, and the remains of an angry welt marked one eyebrow.

For several minutes, Alaina watched the child push the car in circles around the track. Then he rolled the car off the roadway, stopping it next to a small cardboard shoebox on which square windows and a door had been scrawled in brown crayon. Someone had cut along the top and side of the door so it could open and close.

With two fingers, Shaquis walked an imaginary person away from the car and through the tiny door, just big enough for his fingertips to step inside. He pulled the door shut with a *ksh*, then finger-walked a second imaginary person from the car to the box-building. He flicked his fingertips against the closed door as if kicking it with tiny feet.

"Let me in," the boy growled, his voice pitched low.

"Shaquis," Alaina asked gently, "who is kicking the door?"

"That's Damon," he said matter-of-factly. He flicked his fingers against the door again, accentuating each strike with a *ksh* from the back of his throat. "I said, 'Let me in!'"

"Why is Damon kicking the door?"

"He wants my mom to let him in the house."

"Why won't she?"

Shaquis was silent for a moment. "He's not nice."

Alaina absorbed this information for a bit, then reached into her tote for a pad of paper and crayons.

"Shaquis." She leaned down to peer into his face. "Would you like to draw with me?"

The boy looked up for the first time, his chocolate-brown eyes gazing intently into Alaina's. He looked from her to the paper and crayons lying on the floor between them.

Taking that as consent, she opened the box and shook out a few crayons, handing him the orange one. "Can you draw me a picture of your mom?"

The boy took the crayon and scrawled a stick figure on the paper. He scribbled curly hair on the woman, then drew a frown on her face and eyes dripping tears. Alaina stifled a sigh. The pain these little ones felt always sliced at her heart like a knife.

"Why is your mom crying?"

Shaquis shrugged. "She always cryin'."

Opposite the drawing of his mother, he drew another stick figure, fists raised in the air. The second figure also wore a frown.

"Is that Damon?" Alaina whispered.

Shaquis nodded. "He's always yellin'."

She hated asking the next two questions, but it had to be done. "Does he hit your mom?"

The little boy nodded again.

"Is he the one who hit you?"

Another nod confirmed her suspicions.

"Tell you what. Let's play a game." Alaina picked up a

brown crayon, and on a blank piece of paper drew an island surrounded by wavy blue water. Shaquis watched with solemn eyes. She turned the page toward him. "Let's pretend this is an island and you're on it all by yourself. If you could have anyone with you, anyone in the world, who would it be? Can you draw me a picture of who would be there?"

Shaquis bit the corner of his lip. Then, with intense concentration, he used a red crayon to draw a stick figure with curly hair and a wide smile. Next he drew a smaller person, a smile on the round face, holding hands with the larger one. "That's me and my mom."

Alaina opened her mouth to say something, but stopped when Shaquis resumed drawing. A third smiling figure appeared on the island, one stick leg on the ground, the other extending out over the water. Shaquis picked up a yellow crayon and drew sunbeams around the third person's face.

"Who's that?"

"It's the man who stands in the corner of my room every night."

Alaina caught her breath. This was a new knot to untie. It didn't correlate to anything she knew about the boy's case, and her mind ran wild. "That's not Damon?"

"No, Damon's bad." The boy scribbled brown on the base of the island. "This man's good."

Alaina rested her chin on one hand. "How do you know that?"

"When he's there, I ain't a'feared of nothin'. Then I can sleep real good."

Alaina's thoughts drifted back to when she was a small girl. A glowing angel nightlight stood guard on her bedside table every night. Her grandmother had given it to her when she found out Alaina was afraid of the dark. She had told her that it would remind her of the guardian angel who, even though she couldn't see him, stood watch over her bed every night. She hadn't thought about that in years.

She hadn't even been to church lately. In her current job, she saw so many hurting children that she had begun to wonder if there even was a God. If so, how could He allow these little ones to be hurt so badly?

"Miss Alaina?"

Her thoughts plunged back to the present. "Yes?"

"Mama Claire said that even though bad stuff happens, Jesus loves me. Do you believe in Jesus?"

The corners of Alaina's mouth turned up in an almost-smile. She looked into those earnest brown eyes gazing at her, awaiting her response. Such a beautiful, innocent child. She felt a stab of conviction and suddenly knew the answer. How could there not be a God when such purity existed in the world?

"Yes, Shaquis. I do believe in Jesus. And yes, He does love you."

"I thought so." The boy grinned and went back to his cars.

The rest of the visit went pretty much as normal. Alaina talked a bit more with the boy and then with Claire for a while. Once satisfied she had enough information to fill out her report, Alaina excused herself and headed for her car. She started the engine and turned the AC on high, grateful for the cool air blowing against her damp skin.

As she put the car in gear and headed for the freeway, her thoughts remained on her conversation with Shaquis. She still didn't understand why bad things happened to innocent children. But because of one little boy, she knew that there was a God who saw all and who watched over His children.

*Maybe it's time to find some answers.* She pressed the button on the car's hands-free communication system. "Call Jeanette."

The connection made, the phone rang twice on the other end. A woman's voice responded. "Hello?"

"Hi, Mom. It's me. I was thinking maybe I could swing by Sunday morning and we could go to church together. I have a couple of questions I'd like to ask you."

## Life Application

From time to time, things happen in life that we don't understand. Jobs are lost, dear friends and family members pass away, businesses collapse, innocent ones fall into harm's way. We wonder if God really knows what He's doing, if He's actually in control.

These are difficult issues to work through, and they raise questions that are tough to answer. And yet, even when we think God doesn't hear us, He's there—watching, listening, reaching out to us. And when we least expect it, He calls to us, maybe through circumstances, through a Scripture verse, through a friend, and sometimes through a little child.

Children have a unique place in God's heart because they trust—perfectly, completely, and unquestionably. And sometimes God uses them to remind us adults how we should trust Him. With blind trust, like a child's.

Don't forget to listen to the children in your life. They want you to know that God loves you.

## About the Author

**Dona Watson** grew up with books and an imagination full of mystery and adventure. Her fantasy novel *The Lightstone of Perlan* placed in two contests, and her short stories have been published online and in print. You can find her at home in Temecula, California, surrounded by way too many books, or online at DonaWatson.com.

# 14

# Power's Wisdom for an Empty Tank

## by Jeanette Morris

*G*reg Morrison slapped the steering wheel of his BMW and cursed. A dust devil swirled through the cotton fields on either side of the narrow farm road as his out-of-gas sedan sputtered to a stop on the graveled shoulder.

"Recalculating," the mechanical female voice announced.

Greg switched off the GPS and rolled down his window for air. A hot blast of California summer hit him square in the face.

"Fabulous," he muttered. Why did he think this shortcut to Bakersfield would save time? Now his ten-minutes-early arrival would be more like two hours late—if he was lucky. Wondering if there was an emergency vehicle within fifty miles, he reached for his iPhone.

No service. That figured. Why would any self-respecting cellular provider spend money on a tower in this wasteland?

Greg scowled at the cotton bolls collecting on the side of the road. So much for the hot tip that the convention center needed a new insurance broker. Nothing to do now but wait for someone to come along. He adjusted the sun visor, reclined the leather seat, and closed his eyes.

An hour or so later, a distant clattering roused him. Hoping it wasn't just a combine turning over cotton bushes, Greg got out of the car. He raised his hand to shield his eyes from the mid-afternoon glare and looked up the road ahead, then back the way he had come. There, a puff of dust obscured the heat wave rippling across the narrow highway. A long minute later, a beat-up Toyota pickup came into view, slowed, and stopped next to where Greg leaned against his black sedan.

"Need help, señor?" the driver called out the open passenger-side window.

Greg peered at the battered truck and the old Hispanic man behind the wheel—both dusty brown and weathered from the scorching sun. Rivulets of sweat traced crooked lines down the man's wrinkled face. A once-white sombrero slumped around his gray temples.

Greg looked at his watch. Did he have time to wait for someone more … reliable?

"Señor?" the old man prompted.

"Yeah. Well. It seems I'm out of gas. You wouldn't have any back there, would you?" Greg jerked his head toward the bed of the pickup, hoping to slip the guy a few bucks for a quick fix and be on his way.

"Sorry, señor. That's too dangerous in this heat. But I can

take you to Buttonwillow. There's a gas station there."

More bad luck. Everything within him resisted getting into that old truck. Better to wait for the next ... The next what? It could be hours before anyone came by.

"My name is Pablo." The old man smiled. A gold-capped tooth glinted in the sunlight.

He looked innocent enough, except for the tattoos circling his wrists. An ex-con? He didn't seem the type.

Greg swallowed. "All right. Let me lock my car."

"Good idea, señor."

That wasn't assuring, but walking wasn't an option. Nor was waiting any longer. He grabbed his phone and briefcase, locked the car, put his keys in his pocket, and climbed in beside Pablo.

The pickup topped out at about 40 mph. Pablo hummed something off key as they puttered down the back road. Desperate for anything to silence the annoying "music," Greg asked the man about his tattoos.

"These?" He turned over his left wrist, then his right. "I got them when I was young, after the death of my grandfather. To remember him and his favorite story."

Greg wasn't too keen on stories, especially ones told by old guys about times and places that had no relevance today. But Pablo was doing him a favor by taking him into town. And the tale had to be better than the humming. "Okay. Let's hear it."

Pablo nodded and smiled. Clearly, the invitation to spin a yarn pleased him.

"Many years ago, in a fishing village in southern Mexico, there lived a man who had a small rowboat. From time to time, a traveler would arrive and ask to be taken across the lake. The man was glad to oblige, as it earned him a few extra pesos to feed his large family."

Greg licked his drying lips, grimacing at the taste of oily dirt.

"On a particularly warm summer's day, the man took on a passenger. As they approached the middle of the lake, the passenger, while watching the rhythmic splashing of the oars through the water, asked the rower, 'Is that writing I see on your oars?'

"'*Sí*, amigo. One says *trabajo* and the other *suplica*.'

"The passenger took off his hat and scratched his head. '*Work*, I understand. Rowing a boat is difficult and takes strength. But *prayer*?'

"The rower smiled, then pulled the oar carved with *suplica* out of the water. He rowed the other oar with both hands, pulling with all his might. The rowboat turned, then circled. The hot sun beat down, and both men began to sweat.

"'You see,' said the rower, 'hard work is not enough. We are just going in a circle and not making progress. In the sea of life, there are things we can't control. So to reach the shore of this lake, and to have peace within our lives, we need both oars in the water—work and prayer.'"

Greg shook his head. He had tried praying a few times in his life, but God never answered. Hard work, and lots of it, had gotten him where he was today. Nobody had helped him achieve success in life. He had done it on his own.

"You did not like my grandfather's story, señor?"

"No offense, Pablo, but I don't really see the point in praying."

The old man didn't reply. He simply stared out the windshield, as if he were listening to an inner voice.

They rode in silence for a while. The hot air and dust from the open truck windows continued to coat the inside of the rusty dashboard with a layer of brown. Greg's Armani suit would need a trip to the dry cleaners before he could wear it again. Would Buttonwillow have a place he could trust to do it right? Most backwater farm towns had little else than a grocery store, a gas station, and a few bars. Sometimes a Catholic church with a junkyard next to it.

"Uh-oh." Pablo glanced at the dials behind the steering wheel. "She's overheating again."

Greg craned his neck to get a glimpse of the temperature gauge. Sure enough, the dial was well into the red. He shook his head. What else could go wrong today?

Pablo took his foot off the gas, downshifted, and steered toward the shoulder. "Sorry, señor. But I have to pull over. This old girl, she can only do so much." The pickup rumbled over the rough ground, coming to a stop next to a grove of orange trees. Hisses and pops echoed under the hood.

"How long will we have to sit here?" Greg muttered.

Pablo didn't reply. He calmly opened his door, stepped out, and retrieved a rag from behind his seat. Protecting his hands with the cloth, he opened the hood of the steaming truck, then returned to the cab and sat.

"Aren't you going to do something? Add water? Call a tow truck?" Then Greg remembered the cell-service problem.

"I am not a mechanic, señor. I pick cotton, oranges, and olives. I do my job well. But no matter how hard I work, this old truck, she doesn't always work for me." He smiled and raised his right hand. "But I can pray!"

Greg laughed. "Seriously? You really think you can fix an overheated engine with some mumbo-jumbo to the Great Mechanic in the Sky? I doubt God is interested in your problems—or mine."

Pablo closed his eyes, his right arm still lifted, displaying the *suplica* tattoo.

The truck continued to belch white steam. Greg wiped his damp forehead with the back of his hand and searched the orchard for shade. If he was going to sit and wait for a "miracle," he'd rather do it somewhere cooler than the cab of a broken-down farm truck.

"I'm getting out," he announced, and reached for the door handle.

Pablo opened his eyes. He seemed puzzled. "As you wish, señor. But I will be leaving soon for Buttonwillow." He got out of the cab, went to the front of the truck, and closed the hood.

Greg leaned over toward the steering wheel. The temperature needle was still in the red. The old man must be crazy. *Just my luck to get picked up by a religious fanatic.* He blew out another breath of frustration, but stayed in his seat.

Pablo got behind the wheel, closed the door, and turned the ignition key. The engine groaned. He turned it off and patted the top of his dashboard. "There, there, little lady. We are going to be okay. I believe you are ready to get my new friend to town." He turned the key.

The engine groaned again. Then sputtered and came to life.

"*Gloria a Dios!*" Pablo shouted, raising his right hand again. "*Grácias!*" He shoved the transmission into gear and moved off the shoulder onto the road.

Greg checked the gauge. Normal. *What in the world?*

"I see you are surprised that God answered my prayer." The truck lurched when Pablo shifted into third gear. "He does care about us. About small things, like the engine of an old truck. And big things too ... like the doubts in our hearts."

Greg snorted. Coincidences happened to people every day. Good ones, bad ones. It was just fate or luck. Nothing more. Still, this Pablo character really seemed to believe. "How can you be so sure?"

"This life is not easy, so I live by faith, señor. I have little to offer anyone. But what I have, I give to God. Today I asked Him to send me someone who needed to get across the lake. And I believe He did."

A twinge of gratitude punctured Greg's self-sufficiency. It grew inside his chest as they bumped along the road toward town. No other vehicles passed them in either direction. When they pulled in to the gas station, Greg had to admit he would still be sitting in the blistering sun in the middle of nowhere if Pablo hadn't happened by. Maybe this dusty field worker could teach him something after all.

"Got time for a cold one … Señor Pablo?"

The old man nodded. Patted the steering wheel. And began to hum.

## Life Application

The Christian life is most attractive when it is lived out boldly in everyday moments and with ordinary people. In your interactions and relationships with others, are you more like cynical Greg or faith-filled Pablo? Do people see what God is like in the way you treat them? Or do they have to go elsewhere to receive tangible evidence of God's grace and unconditional love? What small change in your attitude toward others can you make today that will better reflect the sacrificial love of Christ?

### About the Author

**Jeanette Morris** is a freelance writer and editor living out her second-half adventure in Atascadero, California, in the Eastern Sierras in her fifth-wheel RV, and in Russia as a part-time missionary. Her publishing credits include articles in *SALT Fresno* and local newspapers, devotionals in *Secret Place* and *Mustard Seed Ministries*, and book reviews for Blue Ink, The Christian PEN, and Thomas Nelson's BookLook Bloggers.

# 15

# The Setting ...
# The Pruning ... The Fruit

by Amarilys Gacio Rassler

Miriam gazed at the vineyard near Young Harris, Georgia, which spread before her, up the mountains, and all around her for as far as she could see. She wanted to take in this beautiful scenery as vividly as she could ... before her light turned to darkness.

Macular degeneration, the doctor's diagnosis. How on earth would she handle it? Fear of blindness drove many decisions now, including the timing for this trip.

Miriam focused on the beautiful setting. The vines, loaded with sun-kissed fruit of different hues, perfumed the wind with the sweet scent of rich, ripened grapes. It wafted through the air while a caressing breeze tossed her hair ever so softly. She let the wind play with her shoulder-length strands of brown streaked by the snows of her life's winter. She would etch in her mind every detail of the place that meant so much to both her and her husband.

She and Dan had visited this vineyard every autumn for as long as either of them could remember.

"You must come in the spring," the owner had said at nearly every visit. "You've seen it when our maple trees blush. But there's nothing like the grapevine's branches pregnant with fruit. It's worth the pruning in January. Heavenly magic!"

She could not put it off any longer. This would be her last chance to see the amazing sight.

Dan gave her a warm smile and stretched his hand toward her. She quickly buried hers into her pants pockets.

Disappointment clouded his eyes. He turned and walked ahead, their black Scottish terrier by his heels, down the path between the two man-made lakes.

As always on a Sunday, the vineyard was void of workers. Not far to her right, Miriam heard the happy chatter of a Tom Sawyer and a Huckleberry Finn, fishing and laughing. Except for the two youths, the grounds were empty.

Just like her heart.

Miriam's chest tightened suddenly, and her steps faltered. As she fell to the ground, she opened her lips to call out, then stopped herself. Her husband was too far away to hear.

The heart palpitations came faster. Her nails dug into her palms. "No, no." She rubbed above her breast and focused on her breathing. In and out. In and out.

The vibrations under her hand finally ceased. Miriam opened her eyes to search for Dan. His back was still to her, his torso curved as if he struggled with an invisible weight. Miriam's eyes filled with tears. Some rolled down to her mouth. She tasted their salt.

She knew the burden her husband carried ... razor sharp, cutting deep. Dan's successful business had required more travel in the years before his retirement, and their empty nest had left Miriam floundering. She'd discovered excitement and a rekindled zest for living in the arms of Dan's best friend.

But conviction disrupted her quiet time with the Lord each morning. After just a few months, she ended the scandalous relationship. But nothing could pare away her self-contempt. Her soul still felt heavy, like a vine laden with dead branches.

She ached for her husband's embrace. Yet months had gone by without her letting him touch her. *You're unclean*, the voices in her head repeatedly insisted.

Miriam unleashed a rush of tears. Her mouth whispered words that her will had been fighting against for the past year. "Oh, God, help me."

Dan stopped, straightened, and turned around. When he saw her crumpled on the ground, he ran to her, stopping abruptly when he reached her side. His face revealed the conflict that raged within him. He longed to help—that was clear. But he wasn't sure how to approach her anymore.

She breathed in deeply, and the tears slowed to a trickle.

Dan pointed to the sky. Then he wrapped his arms around himself, mimicking a hug. Yes, yes, she knew. He'd told her often. God loved her. And so did he.

His face softened, his ruddy cheeks rounded by the curl

of his smile. "Miri," he murmured. He brought his hand to his lips and kissed it. Then he blew the kiss toward her.

Hope fluttered within her heart. Nostalgic thoughts, like photos in a family album, sent her to a sweet-as-honey past. He'd called her by his special nickname only on a few occasions. "Miri," he'd whispered in the afterglow of their first night together. "Thank you, Miri," he'd shouted when he beheld their child for the first time. "Miri, my love," he'd cried as he lay by her side, holding her after her mastectomy.

"Please, Miri." His words trailed through the wind, melting her heart. "Let it go, my love. Let it go." Their little dog barked, echoing his master's plea.

As her husband extended his arms to her, heat sprang into Miriam's heart, dissipating the frost and pruning away her guilt and shame. She rose to her feet, her legs trembling.

Dan drew her into an embrace. "We've both hurt enough. It's over."

She buried her face in his chest, and they wept together.

"We'll manage this together. I promise. No matter what happens, I will love you till the end of time."

He lifted her chin. She stared deep into his topaz-colored eyes, full of mercy and grace. That look would be forever etched in her mind—even more vividly than their lovely setting.

"I've forgiven you, my love." He pulled her tighter to himself. "Now forgive yourself."

## Life Application

When we fall into sin, and then repent and accept Christ's forgiveness, we often continue to reproach ourselves. As a result, we can be tempted to disconnect from our merciful God, as Miriam did. She wondered how on earth she would deal with her coming blindness. Yet within her reach was the help she needed—from heaven. She could forgive herself and cope with her trials simply by coming to her heavenly Father. He tells us in His Word, "If we confess our sins, he is faithful and just and will forgive us our sins and purify us from all unrighteousness" (1 John 1:9). Our God has also promised, "Never will I leave you; never will I forsake you" (Hebrews 13:5).

Trials come into our lives to prune us and bring us closer to God. Miriam found divine grace through her husband's forgiveness and unconditional love. When we have lost our way, God can prune us of the dead branches of guilt and shame if we seek Him, receive His forgiveness, and forgive ourselves. Then we can extend the rich fruit of mercy to others. We can be a beautiful setting that mirrors God's grace.

### About the Author

**Amarilys Gacio Rassler** worked as a volunteer industrial chaplain for the Busch Gardens theme park in Tampa, Florida, for fifteen years. Under the leadership of Busch Gardens vice president Mike Patrick, she led devotionals for the employees. She is the author and facilitator for discussions of the book *The Chairs: A Glimpse into a World Unseen*.

# 16

# Among the Shades of Gray

by Carolyn Bennett Fraiser

Shadows beckoned from down the street. How could she resist their pull?

Nikki picked up the canvas bag stuffed with a stained shirt, muddy jeans, and a fleece jacket two sizes too small. She had kept it hidden in the back of her closet, just in case. They were the only possessions she brought with her whenever she moved into each new home, and the only items she took with her when she left.

Hefting the bag over her shoulder, she crawled out the bedroom window onto the mahogany planks shading the front porch. Many nights she'd enjoyed watching the moon rise above the North Carolina oaks that lined the streets of this historic Charlotte neighborhood. But tonight, she just wanted to climb down the polished trellis and disappear.

Mud squished under Nikki's sneakers as she slid to the ground. There was something comforting about the night.

The darkness didn't judge between black and white. Just like the shadows, girls like Nikki didn't belong in either world. They were stuck somewhere in between, among the shades of gray.

The beige two-story house grew smaller as Nikki scrambled down the street. Coarse brown hair escaped from her French braid and whipped against her cheek. She had to look back, though she couldn't explain why. Nor did she understand why she'd cried so hard when she left the Post-it on her dresser saying simply, "I'm sorry."

Once again, she had ruined everything. Yes, she was mad. But she didn't have to throw her English book at the dresser, breaking the porcelain jewelry box covered with delicate painted roses. Bryan and Christine had given her the gift just one month ago, to celebrate the finalization of her adoption.

"For the treasures you want to keep," Bryan had told her that night. Inside the box, soft red velvet cushioned the edges, promising to protect whatever she laid inside.

Now only fragments remained, reminding her of the damage she had caused her new family.

Life with Bryan and Christine had been fine … until last Sunday, when they insisted she go to youth group instead of sitting in the sanctuary with them. Moments after she entered the classroom, she heard some girls whispering behind her back.

"I can't believe that half-breed showed up here."

"Do you think the Nicholsons will keep her?"

"Not for long. She's nothing but a thief and a liar, you know."

Nikki recognized that voice. The perky brunette had

caught her trying to shoplift a pack of peanut-butter crackers from Walgreens a year ago. She'd snitched to the manager, who called Mrs. Chadwick, her social worker. That was the first week after she came to live with Bryan and Christine.

Anger boiled in Nikki's gut at the girls' cruel comments. So instead of staying in the classroom, she stormed outside to sulk in Brian's SUV.

"Give it time," Christine had said on the way home. "You'll make friends."

Nikki shook her head. "Those girls will never like me, Christine. I'm too different. Please don't make me go back."

Christine's eyes had glistened. "Honey, you can call me Mom now. The adoption is official. No one can change it."

*No one except me.*

Nikki sprinted the next three blocks to the bus station. Walking never provided the distance needed to escape. It only ensured a quick return to the group home, which she hated even worse than the girls at church.

Nikki jumped on the last bus of the evening and slunk into a seat at the back, dropping the canvas bag on the bench beside her.

Since she was three, Nikki had moved from home to home, leaving behind a trail of disaster wherever she lived. She'd broken windows, dented car doors, and run away more times than she could count.

"That girl is a walking time bomb," said Mr. Jackson, one her foster parents, as he dropped her off at the group home when she was nine.

When Bryan and Christine took her in five years later, Nikki didn't expect much. But their home was different from all the others. They laughed at dinner and looked straight into her eyes when they talked to her—like she was a real person instead of a problem child. Christine spoke with a voice as soft as the velvet in the jewelry box. It was never shrill and always in control. Bryan's green eyes twinkled under the shadow of his sandy brown hair. When he smiled, Nikki swore she could count every one of his teeth. After twelve years in the system, she finally belonged. She swore she'd behave this time.

But keeping that promise had proven impossible. She had a violent temper. No amount of prayers could change that. After today, she knew they would send her back—just like the others had.

She needed to go somewhere safe, somewhere familiar, a place where neither Bryan nor Christine would find her.

The driver stopped in front of the rescue mission on the edge of downtown. Nikki grabbed her canvas bag and exited the bus.

A couple of blocks away, she stopped at a familiar nook between two office buildings. This spot, about the size of a small dumpster, was her special place. The brick walls blocked the wind on cold nights, and the deep shadows hid her from people walking by on the street. Finally, she was safe.

After pulling the jacket out of her bag and wrapping it around her, Nikki settled into the corner and closed her eyes.

*They would have taken you back*, a voice in her head suggested.

"It would never last. I'm better off on my own."

Loneliness hung like a wet blanket around her neck, choking her breath. She missed her soft bed, and the crickets chirping outside her window, but most of all, she missed the hugs Bryan and Christine gave her before saying good night.

Tucking her knees under her chin, she huddled in a ball and cried until the tears sucked the last bit of strength out of her body. She collapsed into the shadows and allowed the darkness to swallow her whole.

Nikki woke to tiny, cold raindrops falling on her cheek. Temperatures had tumbled during the night, and although the sky glowed with the promise of morning, the lack of warmth reminded her that winter lingered around the corner. It was a bad time of year to run away.

As her eyes adjusted to the dawdling shadows, Nikki realized she was wrapped in a warm wool blanket, much thicker than the ones volunteers handed out on nights that dipped below freezing. Where had that come from?

In the far corner, a shadow shifted.

Panicked, Nikki mentally retraced the number of steps back to the rescue mission. Even when it was full, they always found a place for her, especially when someone on the street bothered her. But the human shadow, slumped over a piece of cardboard, didn't seem threatening. In fact, it looked vaguely familiar.

A mass of wet, sandy brown hair streaked with ash turned and revealed a pair of twinkling green eyes. "Nikki?"

"Bryan! How—how did you find me?"

He stepped closer. "Mrs. Chadwick told me she thought you might be here."

*Figures.* Nikki's back stiffened. "I'm not going back."

Bryan patted her hand. "You don't have to. We'll find another church, one where you feel comfortable."

"It's not about the church."

"Then where are you afraid to go?"

"The group home, of course." She shrank back into the shadows, but they didn't hide her. She was trapped.

"Nikki, you're our daughter. We would never send you back there."

Tears spilled down her cheeks before she could stop them. "I'm fine here."

"Christine and I want you to come home … with us."

"And if I don't want to?"

Bryan paused for a moment that felt like an eternity. "Then I'll stay here, with you."

"You can't do that. What about your home, your job, and your wife?"

"But what about you?"

"I can take care of myself."

"You're fifteen. Let us do that for you."

Surely Bryan would leave if she pushed him hard enough. "You won't last on the streets."

"I will stay here as long as you do."

"Why?"

"Because I love you." Bryan's eyes glistened, just like they did when he gave her the jewelry box. The one she had shattered. Just like she'd shattered his trust.

Nikki wasn't sure how to respond. "I break things. A lot."

"Things can be repaired." Bryan pulled the porcelain box from his pocket and handed it to her. Nikki's heart sank. The gift was cracked and chipped, but the major pieces had been glued back together. "It's not perfect, but neither are we. We can make this work … if you want to."

Nikki swallowed the bile forming in her throat. "And what if I don't?" She held her breath as he looked into her eyes.

"Then I'll stay here forever."

Forever? He couldn't be serious. Bryan wouldn't give up everything to live in a smelly, cold alley in the worst part of the city. Nikki searched his eyes for any hesitation, but he didn't waver. Bryan always kept his promises. And now he was offering to sacrifice his life just to be with her and keep her safe.

Nikki took a deep breath. "Do you mean that?"

Bryan nodded as tears fell freely down his cheeks.

"Dad? … I really want to go home."

## Life Application

Nikki had access to everything: a home, a warm bed, and a family who loved her. Yet as long as she continued to focus on who she was in the past, she could never truly accept unconditional love.

Sometimes, as Christians, we're tempted to return to an old life, to a place that's familiar and comfortable. But God has so much more in store for us. And He is willing to go with us to the darkest places of our souls to show us how much He loves us.

In Psalm 139, the psalmist wrote, "I can never escape from your Spirit! I can never get away from your presence! If I go up to heaven, you are there; if I go down to the grave, you are there" (vv. 7–8 NLT).

Have you ever tried to run away from God? To what extremes did He follow you? How did He show you His love even in the darkest place of your soul?

## About the Author

**Carolyn Bennett Fraiser** is a freelance writer and journalist with more than eight hundred published articles, devotionals, and short stories in publications, including several titles of Chicken Soup for the Soul. Carolyn lives with her husband, Bruce, and their two cats in Asheville, North Carolina. Follow her on Twitter: @carolynbfraiser.

# 17

# Afraid to Ask

by Jeanette Hanscome

Carrie knocked on the open door to Leanne's classroom. "Ready to work out?"

Her friend tapped her computer mouse a few times. "As soon as I save this."

"Please tell me that's your job application." Carrie had been bugging Leanne to apply for a position at the local college since she spotted the posting two weeks ago. It still baffled her that a woman with a PhD in literature and publishing credits in literary magazines had worked as a sixth-grade remedial English teacher for more than a decade. No wonder she never seemed happy at work.

"Yes, I finished it," she said with a sigh.

"Good for you!" Carrie clapped her hands like a giddy middle-school girl, ignoring the tone in her friend's voice that sounded like a student who had finally finished a dreaded homework assignment. "You're going to send it tonight, right?"

Leanne shoved her keyboard back. "Yeah, probably."

"The deadline's Friday."

"I know. But I'm still thinking about it."

"What's to think about?" Carrie almost shrieked.

Leanne shrugged. "I'm just not sure this job is for me."

Carrie plopped into one of the classroom chairs. "How could it not be? It's exactly what we've been praying for."

"I know it sounds perfect. But is it really wise to leave my secure position here—especially at my age?"

Carrie fought the urge to lay into her friend. How many times had she listened to Leanne complain about how stuck she felt and prayed with her for direction? This was the third job lead she'd sent to Leanne since hearing about her pre-marriage-and-kids dream of being a college English professor. And for the third time, Leanne planned to flake out of the application process. Sure, the woman was in her fifties. But that was no excuse.

Carrie hopped up and nudged Leanne's shoulder. "Change of plans. Forget the workout. We're going out for coffee."

"Aren't you supposed to be holding me accountable to an exercise routine?"

Carrie took her arm. "We'll make it up over the weekend. Today we need to talk."

Leanne groaned. "Okay, *Mom*."

"Hey, I think you need a little mothering today. Meet me at Peet's."

Carrie started praying before she reached her car. It was the only way she could calm her frustrations and prepare to talk to Leanne in a mature, nonconfrontational manner.

*God, give me the words to convince my friend that she's making a big mistake by not applying for this job. I don't think I can listen to any more of her whining.*

She watched Leanne get into her car. Its rusty appearance matched her outdated clothes and rundown apartment.

Carrie had connected with Leanne two years ago, soon after being hired at Lakeside Middle School as an English teacher. They shared a mutual love for teen novels and coffee, and were both single and trying to get back into shape. But sometimes, Carrie didn't get her friend at all. Leanne hadn't received much support from her former husband, so Carrie understood her need to accept whatever job would bring in income. But her kids had been out of the house for more than a year. This seemed like the perfect time to go for what she really wanted.

*Help me understand her, Lord.*

As she started backing out of her parking space, a voice in her head whispered, *Maybe you understand her better than you think.*

Carrie tried to focus on the cars around her. *God, today isn't about me. It's about Leanne.*

*Maybe it's about both of you.*

*Right. Me telling her what You want me to say. So give me the right words for her. Please?*

By the time Carrie found her friend in line at Peet's, she felt ready to say what was on her heart. They ordered their drinks and found a quiet table in a back corner.

Leanne set down her latte, staring at her hands wrapped

around the steaming cup. "You're disappointed in me, aren't you?"

Carrie blew on her mocha. "I just don't understand why you would pass up this great opportunity."

Leanne took a sip as if drawing on the caffeine for strength. "I want that job more than anything." Her voice cracked.

"Then why not go for it?"

Tears welled up in her eyes. "Because I'm … afraid."

Compassion replaced Carrie's desire to play mother. "Why?"

She wiped her eyes with a napkin. "If I send in the application, I'll *really* start wanting that job. And if I don't get it, I'll feel let down."

"I can understand that. You've had a lot of disappointments in your life." Carrie tried to imagine how confident she would feel if her husband had left after twenty years and failed to support the kids he'd brought into the world. Guys like that were the reason Carrie was still single. "But you've been seeking God for new direction, and He has repeatedly sent job leads that fit what you've always wanted. Doesn't it seem like He's opening doors for you?"

"I guess so." Leanne sat back. "You know that Bible verse where Jesus says we're supposed to ask, seek, and knock? And He says, 'Which of you, if your son asks for bread, will give him a stone? Or if he asks for a fish, will give him a snake?'"

"Yeah, of course."

"I guess I've come to expect God to give me stones and snakes."

Carrie chuckled. "Well, it's time to change your expectations."

Leanne wiped away a tear and stared out the window. "I know you're right."

*And what about you? When will you start trusting Me with your desires?*

Carrie fidgeted in her chair. *God, my situation is totally different.*

*Is it?*

The more she thought about her own life, the clearer the similarities between her and her friend became. "Maybe it's time for me to take my own advice," she murmured.

Leanne raised her eyebrows. "You? You're the most confident woman I know."

"When it comes to encouraging others to trust God, yes. But when it comes to my own life, there are some things I'm afraid to even begin seeking God for."

"What is it that you want?" Leanne gently probed.

Carrie's heart caught in her throat. "I want to get married." She couldn't believe she was admitting this after years of claiming otherwise.

Leanne smiled as if she wanted to ask, *Is that all?* "You got somebody in mind?"

"Maybe." Carrie laughed. "A man at church asked me out the other day. Mark's a great guy, and he's never been married."

"And what did you say?"

"I told him I'd think about it."

Leanne shook her head. "Well, let me throw your own

question back at you. What's to think about? Or should I ask, what are you afraid of?"

Carrie ran her fingertip around the edge of her cup. "In high school and college, I attracted a lot of jerks. I couldn't decide if the problem was me or them, so I made up my mind that I was better off single. Now I'm almost forty and I'm starting to want a family—husband, kids, white picket fence, the whole package."

"Maybe Mark is the answer to your prayers."

"That's the thing. I've never had the courage to ask God to send me a husband, or even a date. I guess I'm afraid. I don't want to end up in a bad marriage."

"Like I did?"

Carrie gulped. "No offense, but … yeah."

*Is that really the way you think I work?*

Carrie sucked in her breath, realizing what her attitude said about the God she claimed to love and place her hope in. "You know what, Leanne? I think maybe we have God all wrong. We're acting like He's the one who hurt us. But we know He has our best interests at heart. He's not some bully who dangles what we want in front of our faces only to snatch it away."

Leanne wiped foam off her lips with a napkin. "I want to trust God with my dreams."

"So do I."

"Maybe we should start praying together instead of working out."

Carrie kicked Leanne's foot under the table. "Nice try. How about we pray together *and* work out?"

Leanne grinned. "I knew you'd say that." She drummed her fingers on the side of her cup. "You know what? I'm going to send that application tonight."

Carrie patted Leanne's hand. "Good. And if you don't get the job, it'll be because God has a better one out there for you."

"And the same goes for you and your future husband." Leanne winked. "But you'd better let me be your matron of honor."

"Don't go looking for bridesmaid dresses yet."

The two friends walked out to the parking lot and prayed beside their cars. After a long, warm hug, they said good bye. Carrie felt freer than she had in weeks.

*Lord, thank You for using Leanne's fears to bring out my own. Forgive me for treating You like someone who doesn't care. Help me to see You as the perfect Father who has a wonderful plan to meet every need of my heart.*

## Life Application

As believers, we know that God provides for all our needs and is the source of every good thing. Yet we still hesitate to call on Him for our deepest desires. Why?

Often it comes down to a lack of trust—not based on biblical truth, or even what we know about God, but on the heartbreaks of life. While the Bible teaches about a heavenly Father we can count on to answer prayer and give "good gifts," people hurt us, disregard us, abandon us, abuse us, and lie to us. Assurance that God never breaks His promises is drowned out by the many times when a friend, parent, or spouse did just that. Disappointment after disappointment leaves us afraid of another letdown.

But Jesus urges us to ask for what we desire, to seek Him for the next step, to knock on the door of His throne room. Do we dare take the risk?

The real question is, do we believe that He is a loving Father who wants only the best for His children? Or do we put Him in the same category as those who've shattered our dreams?

Sometimes all we can do is confess our lack of faith and then make up our minds to seek Him, even as our fears rage on. As we learn to place our needs and wants into His hands, we'll see that, even when His gifts don't exactly match the picture we had in our minds, good things come when we have the courage to ask.

## About the Author

**Jeanette Hanscome** has written four published books and many articles and stories. Her most recent work includes the short Christmas fiction e-book *Gifts* and *Running with Roselle* (coauthored with blind 9/11 survivor Michael Hingson). Jeanette lives in the Bay Area and enjoys knitting and crocheting, coffee dates with friends, and being the mom of two amazing sons.

# 18

# Fall from Grace

by Tracy Higley

Vasha clenched her fists and took a deep breath. The heat of the day settled on her like iron chains, dampening her torn dress and sticking dust to her bare feet.

The voice of the auctioneer droned. She studied the young girl on the wooden platform, clothes also ripped and dirty, not more than twelve years old. She sold high. Innocents always did.

The last time Vasha faced a crowd of buyers, she was young, but not innocent. The highest bidder reeked of alcohol and made her regret her "uncooperative spirit." Twice she had become pregnant, but the older slaves always had a remedy.

Last week her master's life of excess caught up with him. Vasha was to be sold.

The auctioneer suggested what services Vasha might perform. His suggestions became explicit and the men cheered. She hung her head.

The auctioneer stepped closer, hand on her dress. Like a lash from a whip, he ripped the fabric to her waist. Bidding began.

It didn't matter who prevailed. She would be mistreated, raped. If her next owner did not beat her to death, she would likely take her own life.

The bids grew sporadic as the price climbed. Moments later, she was shoved off the platform. Bought.

As she waited for her new master to pay the price, Vasha risked a glance. His face had a kindness about it. A small flame of hope flickered.

Hours later, their arrival at his home drew the attention of a beautiful woman at the door. Vasha's owner stepped down and kissed the woman's cheek.

*Men with wives like that don't buy slaves like me.*

A girl a few years older than Vasha joined them. "Welcome home." She kissed the master lightly on the cheek.

*He doesn't look old enough to be her father.*

His attention shifted to Vasha. "This is our newest addition." He reached for her hand.

She hesitated, then put her hand in his and stepped from the wagon.

"Vasha, welcome to our home. This is my wife, and this is Elizabeth. You'll get to know everyone else in time."

Vasha's thoughts spun.

"Come with me." Elizabeth led Vasha toward the house. "I'll show you where you will stay." They walked past rooms of luxury, surely headed to slave quarters behind the house.

Elizabeth began to ascend the back staircase.

Vasha stopped, confused. "Am I to do some work upstairs first?"

"No." Elizabeth laughed. "I'm taking you to your room."

She shook her head. Would she wake up at the auction, purchased by a drunken farmer? She drifted up the stairs, fingers gliding over the banister's gleaming wood.

Elizabeth opened a door in the long hall. "There are clothes hanging there. You can bathe before you change. I'll come for you before dinner."

Vasha stared after her, open-mouthed. Then she turned to the rod of clothes, more beautiful than any she'd ever worn. Rich furniture surrounded a huge bed with a fluffy blanket. Afraid to even sit on the bed, she chose a straight-backed chair with a hard woven bottom and studied the room.

What was this place?

The bed invited, but her clothes were filthy. Her body was just as dirty. Did she dare use the bath?

Ten more minutes slipped by before she peeked out the door. Seeing no one, she grabbed a dress and ran to the small room at the end of the hall.

Basins of steaming water, bars of fresh soap, and soft towels awaited. Several luxurious minutes later, Vasha returned to her room, clean and properly dressed. She succumbed to the soft embrace of the bed.

The sun was setting when Elizabeth knocked and entered.

Vasha jumped to her feet and followed the girl. When Elizabeth led her to a crowded dining table, piled with food, her heart pounded.

*I've slept through the preparations.*

"Welcome, Vasha." Her master pointed to a dark-skinned boy, about ten years old. "The seat next to Amal is for you." All eyes at the table turned toward her.

She hung her head in embarrassment. "I'm sorry, master. Do you want me to serve the food now?"

His wife looked at him in surprise. "Haven't you spoken to her?"

"Not yet." He turned to Vasha. "You're to eat with us tonight. Please, sit down."

Vasha sat, her face flaming. A young woman about her age served the meal. The girl was thanked by everyone at the table and complimented on the meal. Laughter and conversation filled the time, with her master telling stories of his day at the auction. He left out the embarrassing details.

After the meal, Vasha rose to remove the remnants.

"Leave those," her master said. "I want you to come with me."

Her stomach churned. Summoned alone, she knew what was to come.

*I'll never get used to it.*

She followed him into a dark room and waited near the door while he lit the lamp. He indicated for her to take a chair, then sat across from her. Vasha waited for his vile request.

"I know you're confused. Your past experience has taught

you what to expect, but that's not what you have found here. Am I correct?"

She nodded.

"Vasha, you are no longer a slave. It is true that I bought you, but that gives me the right to do whatever I wish with you, and I've decided to set you free."

She raised wide eyes. Set free?

"My wife and I have always wanted children, but that was not to be. So we go to slave auctions and pay the slave price for children. We've done so as many times as we could afford. The young people here are not our slaves; they are our children, and we love them as we would our own."

He paused, but Vasha could formulate no questions.

"I know this must seem strange, but I don't want you for a slave. I want you for a daughter. You will be expected to help with the work of the household, as all my children do, but you won't be forced. If you do not do the work you are given willingly, without complaining, there will be consequences, but you will never be treated as property."

Vasha stared at this strange man.

"Although you are not to be lazy or complaining or ungrateful, you are free to leave at any time." He smiled and stood. "Would you like to go to your room for the night?"

Vasha rose, grateful to escape to the solitude of her thoughts.

At the top of the steps, Amal ran past her with a shy smile and a toy horse in his hand.

Vasha lay awake for hours, thinking about all her master had said. *If I am to believe him, I can't even call him master.*

She had heard the others call him "father." Was that to be her privilege too?

Why had he bought her? Why not the girl before her on the auction platform, or the next girl? How could he not expect her to be his slave after he had paid such a high price for her?

In the days to come, Vasha did any work that was asked of her, anxious to show her gratitude. She worked in the house and in the fields but had an amazing amount of time to herself. Amal began teaching her to read. Evenings became her favorite time, with everyone gathered at the table for dinner and stories and teasing. She finally joined in, telling stories of her own. At night, however, she wondered what it would be like to leave this place and go out into the world, a free woman.

As the weeks went by, the thoughts multiplied.

*If I didn't live here, I wouldn't have to do any work. I could do whatever I chose to do for myself.*

She began to resent some of the work she was given. Why clean up after others, or work in the fields to grow food others would eat? An escape plan took shape in her mind.

Before two months in her new home had passed, Vasha decided to find out what the rest of the world had to offer.

"Hey, beautiful, come over here."

Vasha ignored the grinning man across the street. She

had worked all night and was exhausted. She sat with her back against a building, legs drawn up under her. Even in that huddled position, her profession was evident from her clothes and hair. The man across the street had every reason to call. She simply chose to ignore the potential customer.

She chewed slowly on bread and cheese. They had cost most of her night's earnings, but she had been so hungry, it was worth it. This was her life. Working all night and hiding all day, sleeping and eating.

She was free. She was no longer a slave.

She was a prostitute.

Was it better working for herself instead of in slavery? The result was the same. At least when she had been a slave, she was always sure of her next meal. Now she had to worry about sleeping with enough men during the night to make it through the next day.

She sold herself now. No one else did the selling. But her life was as filled with misery as it had ever been. No one cared for her. Her freedom had not brought her happiness.

Or had it?

*I once belonged to a family.*

She had been given responsibility, but she'd also been given love, respect, and purpose. Now she had put herself in another kind of bondage, almost worse than the first.

"You will never return to being treated like a slave. You will always be a daughter." His words rang in her ears as if she had just heard them. Could they still be true?

Could she ever go back?

## Life Application

Of all the analogies used for our redemption, is there any more emotional than adoption? God did not find us scrubbed clean, dressed in our Sunday best, waiting for an adoptive father. We were led out of a slave market, chains hacked from our ankles and wrists, the filth of guilt washed from our bodies, and brought into the family of God. This was grace, unmerited favor, on spectacular display.

In our life after grace, our bondage to sin is broken. It's a Cinderella story if there ever was one. From rags to riches, from hell to glory.

We never hear of Cinderella returning to scrubbing floors, and yet how many of us choose to return to a focus on ourselves? We go back to old priorities, rejecting the life of grace God has purchased for us.

To believe the paradox of dying to self, we must trust our Father implicitly. He never asks anything of us that would lead outside the life of grace He bought for us. And there is only one way to trust someone. You must know him well.

No matter how far we stray, we can always go back. He waits to welcome us home.

## About the Author

**Tracy Higley has** authored twelve novels, including *The Queen's Handmaid* and *Awakening*. She holds a master's degree in ancient history and has traveled through Greece, Israel, Turkey, Egypt, Jordan, and Italy, researching her novels and falling into adventures. See her travel journals and more at TracyHigley.com.

# 19

# Thorns

## by Nanette Thorsen-Snipes

Amy's stomach lurched when she heard her husband's voice on the cell phone.

"Come back home, honey," he said.

Tears welled in her eyes, but she wiped them away, refusing to let even one trickle down her face. "We're through, Josh." She finger brushed ash-brown hair from her forehead. "I'm not coming back unless you get help." She tapped the phone, ending the call.

Amy returned to browning ground beef for spaghetti for her and her girls. She'd made the right decision by leaving Josh. Since then she had celebrated two months of freedom, with a new job in the metro area. The single-wide mobile home fit their lifestyle. And her friends from church could now visit without fear of being verbally attacked.

The peace she felt was like a placid lake at sunrise, all nice and quiet before the fish stirred and the birds chirped.

Roscoe, her Chihuahua, rubbed against her leg, triggering a memory. Josh had come into the kitchen one day, holding a ripped pillow. The veins in his neck stood out like ribbed cords, and his face was flushed; his brown eyes had a wild look. She knew he'd been drinking.

"Where's that stupid dog?" he shouted. "He tore a hole in my pillow! I want him out of here!"

Amy turned in time to see the dog scamper under the sofa. Josh dove after him.

"You stupid little …" He picked up the dog by the scruff of its neck. She watched in horror as he lifted the animal in the air and shoved open the back door. Before she could stop him, he drop-kicked Roscoe into the yard. The dog yelped.

"Leave him alone!"

"So you'd rather I hit you?"

"You wouldn't dare!" Those three words started the fighting that continued most of that night. By morning, her face was bruised where he'd slapped her, and both arms revealed fingerprint bruises. The memory still chilled her.

Amy rubbed her bare arms. She bent to give Roscoe a reassuring pat. Though she felt pangs of loneliness, she refused to enter into any new relationships. She couldn't trust men. Right now, she even distrusted the God she was learning about in church. But she continued attending services, hoping she would get to know Him better.

She drained the ground beef, then cut up an onion while her two little girls played in the front yard.

Roscoe's insistent barking demanded her attention. When

she opened the back door to let him out, she found Josh standing in the doorway. She gasped. He'd always had a way of sneaking up and startling her. His six-foot-three, well-muscled body filled the door frame.

She attempted to shove the door closed, but he elbowed his way in.

"Amy, I'm sorry." Smiling, he handed her a bouquet of daisies.

"I don't want those, Josh. Just leave."

"Can't we sit down and talk?"

"There's nothing left to say."

Ignoring her rebuff, Josh ambled to the tan leather sofa. He dropped the daisies on the coffee table and sat down.

Amy studied him. She noticed how handsome he looked in his ribbed black tank top and khaki Dockers. His sandy-colored hair flopped across his brow, making him look boyish. For a moment, he reminded her of when they first met, and how polite and considerate he'd been. He had brought her flowers then, too, and she'd thought he was terribly romantic.

Amy sat across from him while he talked about his friends, his new life, and the new woman at his job. "Yeah," he continued, "Sherry's nice. And real pretty. Got long blonde hair, kinda like yours." After a second's hesitation, he added, "But she's not you."

When Amy didn't respond, he started nervously flipping through the pages of the Bible she kept on her coffee table. "Do you read this stuff?"

She looked away, trying to avoid any conversation. "I think you'd better go."

"Not until you promise to see me again." He clasped his hands behind his head, making no effort to leave.

One of the girls flung open the front door. "Daddy!" she hollered, then ran to him. He opened his arms and gathered her in.

"I've missed you, sweetheart. I didn't see you outside." He tousled the little girl's hair. "Where's Kelly?"

"She's probably next door," Amy said.

*He seems so laid back. Maybe he has changed.*

"Are you and Mommy happy again?" Coni asked, her face beaming. "Are we going back home?"

"I don't know, honey. It's up to Mommy."

Two small dimples popped out when Coni smiled, but when she heard her sister calling, she crawled off his lap and ran back outside.

Josh's brown eyes flashed mischievously. "So, how 'bout you get someone to watch the kids, and we'll go out for lunch."

"I don't think so." Amy stood and headed for the door.

He beat her to it and barred the way. "I'm not going anywhere until you promise you'll see me."

"I said no. Now, please leave."

He reached around her and locked the deadbolt.

Fear crouched in Amy's heart like a gazelle pursued by a determined lion. She took a shallow breath and held it a moment. "Okay, let's talk." She hoped he hadn't noticed the way her voice quivered.

He walked back to the couch, sat down again, and patted the cushion beside him. "Come here."

She settled into a wingback chair across from him. "What do you want to talk about?"

"You're too far away, baby. Come sit beside me."

When she stayed put, he got to his feet. Her heart pounded and the blood pulsed in her ears. She eased out of the chair and backed away, one step at a time. Just as she reached the door, he lunged.

Clutching her wrist, he yanked her to the couch and forced her to sit beside him. "There, isn't that better?"

She felt trapped. Fear heaved inside her with every breath.

He leaned close to kiss her, but she turned away. "You need help, Josh."

She wrenched free and again raced to the door. She managed to unlock the deadbolt before he grabbed her arm and whirled her around. She flailed with every ounce of strength she could muster. He slapped her across the face. Hard.

She screamed, holding her burning cheek. She stared at him in disbelief.

"I'm not the one who needs help," he shouted. "You're the hopeless one."

Heat seared her face, but his words ripped at her heart. *Is he right? Am I hopeless?*

His eyes filled with rage, and he balled up his fist. Amy raised her hand to protect herself, but he still managed to punch her.

She crumpled to the floor. A black curtain descended, and

brilliant pinpoints of light flashed in her brain. She crawled toward the chair. When she rose to one knee, he hit her again. His fingernail caught the side of her mouth, and she tasted blood.

"You're a stupid, worthless piece of trash!" Josh turned around, unlocked the door, and charged outside.

Sitting on the floor alone, she sobbed. *Where are You, God? Have You forgotten me?*

When the girls came in, Amy held them close. Kelly and her sister punctuated Amy's sobs with questions, but all Amy could do was put one finger to her lips, willing them to hush.

Later that day, she filed a restraining order.

At church the following Sunday, her best friend asked about the bruises. Amy dodged the question while silently pleading with God for help.

While the pastor led the congregation in the invitational, she felt a tug on her heart. She clutched the pew in front of her until her knuckles whitened. *How can I trust You, God? I can't trust anyone, not even myself.*

The pastor preached on the parable of the prodigal son and the father who openly welcomed him back. As she listened to the theme of forgiveness, Amy wondered if she could ever forgive Josh. She hated him and how worthless he made her feel. She knew her thoughts weren't very godly, but that was how she felt.

As the pastor concluded his sermon, he offered the congregation a suggestion. "If you're unable to forgive someone face to face, place a chair in front of you and pretend the person who has hurt you is sitting there. Speak to them honestly.

Tell them how much you've been hurt, yell at them, cry, whatever it takes. Then forgive them."

Amy blanched at the thought of forgiving her abusive husband.

The next week, she was back in the same pew. When the choir sang the final hymn, she struggled to release the back of the pew in front of her. *Father, I want to come to You, but I can't.* Another week passed before Amy released her firm grip. *Father,* she prayed, *I ask You to give me the strength to forgive Josh.* She opened her eyes and walked forward.

Even after praying with the pastor at the altar, Amy didn't feel any different. But weeks later, she fell to her knees in her bedroom. Her chest constricted as words poured from the depth of her soul. "Father, please release all this hate I have for Josh. Help me forgive him."

She placed an empty chair across from her bed, and sitting on her bedspread, she spoke to the empty chair as though Josh sat there. Her voice trembled. Tears trickled down her face. "You don't know how much I've hated you for what you did to us. You caused us so much pain." Sobs bubbled up.

When her weeping subsided, she wiped her damp cheeks with the back of her hand. Peace flooded her heart and mind. She stared at the empty chair. "Josh, I am releasing you to God. You are in His hands now. Through Jesus, I'm forgiving you for what you've put us through."

Amy stood and looked at her reflection in the mirror. Tears stained her blotchy face, but she seemed to stand taller than ever. Much taller.

## Life Application

Like the apostle Paul, who pleaded with God to remove the thorn from his side, Amy learned she was only strong when she was weak. Until she met the Lord, she was unable to understand the concept of forgiveness. Her biggest weaknesses—believing she could handle everything herself and her inability to forgive—turned into God's opportunity to do something extraordinary in her life.

In Paul's case, God did not remove the thorn, but instead made Paul strong in spite of his weakness. "He said to me, 'My grace is sufficient for you, for my power is made perfect in weakness.' Therefore I will boast all the more gladly about my weaknesses, so that Christ's power may rest on me. ... For when I am weak, then I am strong" (2 Corinthians 12:9–10). By surrendering her life to Jesus, Amy became strong too.

### About the Author

**Nanette Thorsen-Snipes** has published more than five hundred articles, columns, and reprints in more than forty publications and fifty-five compilation books, including stories in three *Guideposts* anthologies in the Miracles series (2007–08), in *The New Women's Devotional Bible* (Zondervan, 2006), and in *Grace Givers* (Integrity House, 2006). She lives in north Georgia with her husband, Jim. They have four grown children and eight grandchildren. Find her at FaithWorksEditorial.com.

# 20

# The Mask

by DiAnn Mills

Rachel stared out her bedroom window at her elderly parents fussing over the hybrid roses in the backyard. As an only child, she'd spent countless hours in solitude. She didn't know what it was like to have brothers and sisters, or parents who were not assaulted by rheumatism and clogged arteries. But she accepted her life without much reservation.

She plopped onto her white chenille bedspread. Rachel knew her parents loved and cherished her, as she did them. But most children her age avoided her. She had been cursed with a cleft palate, a hideous twist of nature that made her the source of cruel teasing. To make matters worse, her teeth had grown in twisted, giving her a speech impediment. The combination caused her to look and sound like a deformed animal.

Rachel no longer sought friendships; the pain of rejection had stung too often. Instead, she delved into books, escaping the trauma of her woeful existence by transplanting herself into faraway worlds.

Rachel's parents had paid for multiple oral surgeries, extensive orthodontic work, and endless speech therapy. She still looked pathetic, with a crooked, dented mouth framing perfectly straight teeth. But at least she could finally talk distinctly.

One day, her parents decided they all needed to attend church together. Perhaps they thought God could turn their ugly-duckling daughter into a lovely swan. She learned that God was known for performing miracles, and she desperately needed one. Oh, to wake up one morning and see a reflection of a normal girl. But it never happened.

When her parents became born again, Rachel attributed it to their advancing age and a desire to "make peace with God."

One Sunday Mom announced, "Your dad and I found a great small-group class at church. Maybe you will too."

"Count me out. I get enough ridicule at school."

Disappointment etched her mother's face.

Some of the kids at church invited her to youth functions, but Rachel knew the invitations rose from a sense of duty. She was certain they laughed behind her back like all the others.

Rachel knew her parents and their new friends prayed for her. The thought bothered her. God had played a cruel joke on her. Why would she want to talk to Him?

Rachel focused on school classes that would train her for a career that had minimum contact with people: accounting, writing, or computer science.

When high school graduation came, Rachel convinced her parents to let her skip the ceremony. The idea of parading across the stage to receive a diploma sent shivers to the ends of her toes. College frightened her even more. She decided to attend a local university and major in computer science.

Six weeks before college began, her parents asked her to attend a play at church with them. She refused, claiming a desire to watch a TV program. She stayed home and wallowed in self-pity.

That night, the phone rang with tragic news. En route home from the play, a drunk driver had collided with Rachel's parents' car. They were killed instantly.

For several days she forgot to eat. She neglected to bathe. She didn't answer the phone or the door.

*God, how could You let this happen? Do You despise me that much?*

Thick clouds cast a gray haze over the hot July days, increasing her vile mood. People from church left food and notes on the front porch. She ignored the gifts.

One afternoon, the doorbell rang. Why couldn't people leave her alone in her grief?

Rachel ignored the bell, but it rang again. On the third ring, she swung open the door, determined to get rid of the persistent intruder.

Her nostrils were immediately assaulted by a horrible smell. She glanced at the garbage around her feet. Ants crawled over the spoiled remains.

As Rachel raised her eyes, she saw a girl about her age. Rachel vaguely remembered her attempting conversation at church. She held up a paper bag bearing the logo of a nearby deli.

"I'm Nicole," she said, her lips quivering. "I wanted to stop by to offer my sympathies … and see if I could do anything for you."

Rachel gritted her teeth and kept her arms glued to her sides.

Nicole smiled, but her eyes pooled with tears.

*Why is she crying?* Rachel wanted to shout obscenities and order her off the doorstep. Instead, her own eyes filled with tears.

Nicole glanced down at the rotted food. "I guess you haven't been hungry."

Rachel shook her head.

"Would you like to try this?" She lifted the deli bag. "It's turkey."

Rachel's stomach growled. Against her better judgment, she reached for the bag. "Thanks."

"You're welcome." Nicole smiled. "Can I stop by again tomorrow?"

"Why?"

"Because I need you."

Nicole's words irked Rachel. Had she become a church project, right up there with the homeless and neglected?

A shaky smile graced the girl's rosebud-shaped mouth. "I don't know what I'd do if something happened to my parents."

"You don't have to feel sorry for me."

Nicole's shoulders drooped. "Oh, Rachel, sympathy is part of love. It's what God wants us to do for others. And I do need you … to show me how to be unselfish."

"What?"

"Your parents taught my Sunday school class. They always talked about you, saying what a wonderful, talented person you are."

What had Mom and Dad said to make this girl think she had anything to offer anyone?

"Enjoy your sandwich. I'll be back tomorrow at one thirty." Nicole hurried down the sidewalk to a little blue sports car. She turned and waved, but Rachel refused to respond.

Sitting at the kitchen table, where she'd shared meals with her parents since the first time her mother scooted the high chair next to it, Rachel ate the sandwich, savoring every bite. She really was hungry.

The following morning, her stomach fluttered. Would Nicole visit? Did she want her to? She truly didn't know. But after breakfast, Rachel bathed and washed her hair. She ran the vacuum and cleaned up the mess on the front porch.

At precisely one thirty, the doorbell rang. Inhaling deeply, Rachel opened the door.

Nicole grinned. "I brought you a book about English gardens. Your mother said you loved to read about faraway places."

Rachel's hand shook as she accepted the gift. "Thank you. I'm glad you came. Would you like to come in?"

That gesture began a close friendship. In the following weeks, Nicole gave Rachel a new perspective on Christianity.

Finally Rachel asked Jesus into her heart. She forgave the drunk driver who had killed her parents. She even learned how to forgive herself.

"I was selfish," Rachel told Nicole as they climbed the university steps for the second semester of classes. She'd changed her major from computer science to special education. "But God did an incredible work in my life."

"I'll say." Nicole grinned. "Your work with deaf and blind children and assisting with the special-ed class at church show a spirit of true giving."

"Who would have thought the Lord could use a selfish taker like me?" Rachel whispered, opening the door of the huge building. "I guess God did."

## Life Application

It's easy to sit alone in a comfort zone and not reach out to others. Becoming involved in someone's problems means we must feel their pain. The effort can sap our energies and pull on our time until we are mentally, physically, and emotionally drained. Sometimes the act takes such a toll we refuse to become involved with anyone again.

Other times, reaching out to others is simply an annoyance; we don't want to be bothered. We have our own agendas, which do not include deviating from our schedules. Family responsibilities, jobs, hobbies, and even ministries are used as excuses not to give to others. We're not proud of our stand. In fact, it needles at our conscience until we reluctantly give in to the pressure or make some justification to avoid the situation.

Blessings come from adversity, and unless we are involved with others we will never discover the joy of true giving.

God wants us to become woven into the lives of others, whether they are Christians or nonbelievers, pleasant or rude, society's finest or the outcasts. His grace extends to everyone, and ours should too.

## About the Author

**DiAnn Mills** is a best-selling author who believes her readers should expect an adventure. She has won two Christy Awards and has been a finalist for the RITA, Daphne Du Maurier, Inspirational Readers' Choice, and Carol award contests. DiAnn loves to connect with readers on any of the social media platforms listed at DiannMills.com.

# 21

# There and Back

by Lori Freeland

The last two miles of the trip were the worst.

Not because the 30 mph speed limit challenged Ellie's lead foot. Or because there were more deer crossings than pedestrian crosswalks in Windsor, Wisconsin. No, the miles hit hard because every farm she drove by, every neighborhood she passed, held a chest of locked up memories that tore at her heart.

She took a right off Highway 19. The weathered giant mouse crouching on top of the Cheese House marked her almost home. Ellie clenched her fingers around the steering wheel. No. Not home. Not anymore.

This tiny town, with its population of three thousand people and twice as many cows, hadn't been home in ten years. She lived in St. Paul now, in the garden condo she'd soon be sharing with Jon.

The large diamond on her left hand sparkled in the

sunlight. Good job, Ellie. Flaunt your engagement in front of Dane's parents. She twisted the diamond around, but the band still screamed wedding, hope, future.

All things Dane would never have.

Maybe she should have let Jon come. He'd offered to drive her. She'd told him no. She had to do this on her own. She'd ripped a hole in Dane's family alone. She had to try to make it right alone. And if Dane's parents chose to withhold their forgiveness, it was what she deserved.

The ribbon-cutting ceremony, the reason she'd come, began at 1:00. She'd sit in the back. Pray she didn't implode. Tell Dane's parents what she'd come to say. Then she'd drag herself back to the hotel and cry. She had a plan. Plans were good. Plans kept her from falling apart.

Not anxious to reach her destination, she swung into the A&W drive-through and ordered a diet root beer.

The cashier's palm shot out the window. "That'll be one dollar and six cents."

Ellie jerked her head up at the familiar voice. "Lydia?"

"Ellie?" Lydia Palmer leaned out the window and took in Jon's cherry-red Porsche. Her nametag read *Lydia Jenkins*. Still blonde, blue-eyed, and lean, she'd barely changed.

Unprepared for this face-to-face with her former best friend, Ellie gripped the gearshift.

"You're here for the ceremony." Lydia's voice dropped.

"Yeah." Sick feelings peeled Ellie's stomach inside out, making her regret the Cajun breakfast. She flattened her hand over the waistband of her black silk skirt. "You and Jim—?"

"We bought the old A&W." Lydia's halfhearted laugh came with a weak grin. "I fill in for no-show employees."

Forcing her fingers not to tremble, Ellie handed over two dollars.

"Nah. It's on me." Lydia gave her the root beer.

Ellie glanced at Lydia's bright red nails topped with gold glitter and then at her own smoky purple manicure. They still shared an addiction to wild nail polish.

For a second, the curtain of years parted and Lydia became Ellie's other half again. In high school they looked so much alike and spent so much time together, Lydia filled in as the sister Ellie never had.

"Sweetie, if you need someone to sit by, find me." Lydia's eyes grew shiny.

Ellie nodded and sat there a moment before she put up her window and drove away. How many other people would recognize her? She should turn around. Drive back to Jon. Pick out a wedding dress. Order their cake.

But she couldn't.

Guilt was a malicious master. He gave no sick days, no vacations, no time-outs. And the longer Ellie stayed bound to him, the more he gnawed off chunks of her soul. No matter how hard she tried to build a life, she couldn't move on.

Why should she? Dane couldn't move on.

She should've listened that night instead of screaming at him for being selfish and stomping away. Sick of his bouts with depression, she'd wanted to celebrate high school graduation. Go to parties. Have fun. Not talk Dane off the ledge.

Again. And she'd paid for that split-second decision not to rescue him—with a decade of regret that crushed her chest like wet cement.

Somehow, Jon's Porsche ended up parked on the narrow pavement inside the cemetery and Ellie ended up on her knees in the grass in front of Dane's grave.

Dane had liked to wander through the headstones, wondering how each person lived. Had Samuel Kline or Martha Benedict or Gerald Grey been happy more days than they were sad? Or had the world felt like a dark place for them, like it was for Dane?

The first time Ellie had come here was on a dare from him in the eighth grade. That night they shared their first kiss—her first kiss—in front of a cracked tombstone marked Hammerly Hurlebutt.

Hilarious in eighth grade. Not so much now that Dane's permanent address stood only a few plots over.

Eyes stinging, she traced his name and the dates etched on the stone. Eighteen years. He would never be more than a teenager. Because she'd let depression steal his future. She might as well have buried him herself the night she abandoned him to party with her friends.

After Dane died, she'd run away to St. Paul, gone to college, and gotten her PhD in clinical psychology. Too late, she earned the degree that could have helped Dane.

"I'm so sorry, Dane." Ellie leaned her forehead against the cold stone. "If I could go back—"

"Ellie?" A soft whisper came from behind her.

She whipped around.

Charlotte bent to her knees, looking almost the same as she had the day Ellie left.

No. Not Dane's mom. Ellie couldn't face her. Not here, in front of his grave.

"I'm glad you came," Charlotte said.

Ellie snagged a breath. "How can you be glad?" She slid her left hand behind her back, hiding the ring.

Charlotte's gaze followed Ellie's hand. "Tell me about your guy." No anger hung in her tone. No condemnation.

"I can't." Tears fell from Ellie's eyes onto the grass. "I don't deserve . . ."

"What? Love? A life?"

"No. Not when Dane—" Ellie's lungs shriveled.

Tugging Ellie's hand forward, Charlotte turned her palm over and stared at the huge, sparkling diamond. And smiled.

Why would she smile? Where was the bitterness? The accusations?

Ellie pulled her hand away. "I came back here to ask you to forgive me. But I don't deserve your forgiveness. I deserve a plot next to Dane."

"Honey." Charlotte pulled her close. "There's nothing to forgive. You were seventeen. Dane's death wasn't your fault."

Lifting her head, Ellie stared at Dane's mom through a blur of tears. "We had all these plans." Her shoulders shook. "I thought he'd get over losing the football scholarship. He didn't even want to play football. It was just a way to pay for college." Her words were a muffled mess, but she couldn't stop talking.

"He was Dane Fuller. Popular, sweet, perfect. Why couldn't that be enough for him?" She drew in a threadbare breath. "Why couldn't I be enough for him?"

"Dane struggled with darkness. You know that." Charlotte squeezed her, and then sat back in the grass. "When I found him that morning, my heart ripped open. I blamed myself. I didn't understand his depression. I didn't get him the help he needed." Her eyes got teary too.

"I should've saved him." Ellie rocked back and forth.

"No." Charlotte put her hand on Ellie's knee. "It wasn't your job to save him. Or mine. Dane chose to take his life." She wiped her eyes and then brushed Ellie's tears from her cheeks. "Do you believe in God, honey?"

Ellie nodded. She'd met Jon at a Bible study he led. But she couldn't tell Charlotte that.

"Do you believe God can redeem the worst moment in our lives and make it beautiful?" Charlotte's eyes held pain, but they also held hope.

"I don't know." How could God cause anything good to come from the way she'd let Dane down? If she hadn't been so selfish. If she'd put Dane first.

"Those first days were hard." Charlotte gazed off into the distance. "Impossible, really. Planning the funeral. Going through old pictures. Realizing I'd never sit at my son's wedding, never hold my grandchildren, never—"

"I'm so sorry."

"I know." Charlotte looked back at Ellie. "But after I met the Lord, everything changed. I changed. I realized I had a choice. I could let my son's death destroy me or allow God to turn it into a miracle. I decided to trust Him. And He brought about that miracle. He healed my breaking heart."

"So you don't hate me?"

"No, honey. But I think you hate yourself. And that's a horrible way to live." Charlotte stood and tugged Ellie up with her. "I want you to do something for me."

"Anything."

"It's gonna be hard." Charlotte reached for Ellie's hand and twisted her engagement ring so the diamond was no longer hidden. "I want you to forgive yourself."

Ellie's vision blurred.

"It means a lot that you came here today. I hope to see you at the ceremony." Charlotte kissed her on the cheek and walked away.

The parking lot was full of people and folding chairs. Ellie slid into an empty seat next to Lydia. Neither of them said a word.

Dane's parents held hands in front of a huge purple ribbon attached to the front door of the old post office. Charlotte stood behind a microphone. "From the time he was little, all Dane wanted was to help people. And now he can."

Dane's dad raised a giant pair of scissors. "Welcome to Dane's Den, a free walk-in counseling center for teens."

Ellie's guilt flared, but she focused on the blue letters on the sign bearing Dane's name and thought of all the kids who would find help here. Sure enough, just as Charlotte said, God had taken Dane's death and turned it into something amazing.

Her restless heart quieted, and some of the cement weighing her down cracked away. For the first time in ten years, she felt peace about her past and hope for her future.

## Life Application

Is there something in your past that has refused to let you move on? Have you felt like forgiveness was impossible? That you needed to pay for your sins forever?

That's not God's voice holding you back. Our loving heavenly Father wants us to be free. That's why He sent His Son to pay for our sins. All of them. Past, present, and future. Don't listen to the dark master of guilt. We aren't chained to his lies. We are meant for light, truth, and peace. We are meant for grace.

Isaiah 26:3 tells us, "You will keep in perfect peace those whose minds are steadfast, because they trust in you." Trust in the Lord. Let Him be the master of your life. Let Him fill you with His light and promise. Give your guilt to God, and He will unshackle you.

God's forgiveness is waiting. It always has been. Go to Him, fall at His feet, and soak up His grace. And then turn around and pass on His mercy to others.

## About the Author

**Lori Freeland** is a writing teacher and coach for the North Texas Christian Writers and a contributor to Crosswalk.com and Believe.com. She's addicted to flavored coffee and imaginary people. When she's not writing inspirational articles, she's working on several young-adult novels. Visit her website, LAFreeland.com, or look for L. A. Freeland on Facebook.

# Closing

$\mathcal{J}$f you've been impacted or blessed by any of the stories in this book, may I encourage you to share that experience with others? Visit our website, FictionDevo.com, and find the forum for "21 Days of Grace." There you can read what others have posted as well as write something yourself about what a particular story meant to you.

If you prefer a more casual setting, visit our Facebook page, facebook.com/FictionDevo, and share your thoughts there.

If this book has sparked a desire in your heart to know God more deeply, or to experience His grace in a personal way, please pursue that longing. The Lord knows your thoughts, and He understands how you feel. He wants to have a close relationship with you, His beloved child.

Don't know where to start? Just talk to Him like you would with a special friend. You can also learn more about Him by reading His book. If you haven't read the Bible much, you may want to start with a contemporary version, such as the ones mentioned on the copyright page of this book. Or visit a local Bible-based church and speak with a pastor there.

If you have any friends who know God in an intimate way, ask them to share their experiences with you. Christians love talking to people about what the Lord is doing in their lives.

God's grace really is amazing. I pray that you will experience it for yourself … every single day of your life!

—Kathy Ide

## Coming Soon

Look for more books in this series
from BroadStreet Publishing

21 Days of Christmas:
Stories of God's Greatest Gift

21 Days of Love:
Stories that Celebrate Treasured Relationships

21 Days of Joy:
Stories that Celebrate Motherhood

# Alphabetical List of Contributing Authors

Roxanne Anderson, "The Pain Redemption"

Robin Bayne, "The Smallest Gift"

Barbara Curtis, "Promptly at Seven"

Diane Simmons Dill, "Be Grateful in All Things"

Carolyn Bennett Fraiser, "Among the Shades of Gray"

Lori Freeland, "There and Back"

Jeanette Hanscome, "Afraid to Ask"

Tracy Higley, "Fall from Grace"

Angela Elwell Hunt, "True Confession"

Kathy Ide, "Rag Doll"

Kathi Macias, "A House with Pillows"

DiAnn Mills, "The Mask"

Jeanette Morris, "Rower's Wisdom for an Empty Tank"

Cecil Murphey, "We Called Him Happy Face

Deborah Raney, "Prairie Lessons"

Amarilys Gacio Rassler, "The Setting … The Pruning … The Fruit"

Buck Storm, "A Waffle Stop Story of Love and Pistols"

Nanette Thorsen-Snipes, "Thorns"

Dona Watson, "The Least of These"

Nancy Arant Williams, "The Guilty Party"

Cindy Woodsmall, "Through a Dark Glass"